SHAVER

ALLEN & UNWIN
FICTION

Susan Geason was born in Tasmania, and has ended up in inner-city Sydney via Brisbane, Toronto and Canberra. With an MA in political theory from the University of Toronto, she has been a journalist with the National Times and a policy adviser in Parliament House, Canberra and the NSW Premier's Department. She is now a freelance researcher, writer and speechwriter working for governments and private enterprise.

SHAVED FISH

SUSAN GEASON

ALLEN & UNWIN

Acknowledgements
For the title, thanks to John Lennon via Frank Frost

© Susan Geason, 1990
This book is copyright under the Berne Convention. No reproduction without permission. All rights reserved.

First published in 1990
Third impression 1992
Allen & Unwin Pty Ltd
9 Atchison Street, St Leonards NSW 2065

National Library of Australia
Cataloguing-in-Publication entry:

Geason, Susan, 1946–
Shaved fish.

ISBN 0 04 442274 1

I. Title
A823.3

Set in 10½/12 pt Goudy Old Style, by SRM Production Services, Malaysia
Printed by Australian Print Group, Maryborough, Victoria.

Cover design: Clea Gazzard
Series design: Peter Schofield
Internal design: Trevor Hood

Double Jeopardy, *Heaven Sent*, *The Pornographer's Son*, *Semi-Precious*, and *Two Dog Night* have appeared in Australian Penthouse.

For my father, my brother, Kath,
Greg, and John Lennon, who
all left too early, and for Lorraine.

Contents

Double Jeopardy	1
Heaven Sent	11
The Pornographer's Son	24
Two Dog Night	44
Semi-Precious	59
Fish Sauce	75
Wasted Lives	90
The Bum's Rush	110
Loco Parentis	123
Boom Town Blues	146

DOUBLE JEOPARDY

The door was opened by Luther Huck, a fat man with a grudge.
'I'm trying to find a wife,' I said.
'That's funny,' he said. 'Most of the punters who come here are trying to lose theirs.'
'Not mine, somebody else's.'
'Sounds better already,' he replied. Neither of us had smiled during this exchange.
'I'm looking for Barry Cromer's wife,' I said.
The bouncer's eyes narrowed, if that were possible: Cromer was Opposition Spokesman on Employment and Industrial Relations — and on morals, manners and motherhood, none of which he'd experienced first-hand.
'Shit, she wouldn't be caught dead in a dump like this,' he said.
'Luther,' I chided. 'It's unlike you to belittle your place of employment.'
I pulled out a photograph of Margaret Cromer and flicked it at him. 'Good looker,' he commented. 'In a ladylike kind of way. We don't get many ladies at Ridge's.'
'If you do,' I said, handing him a fifty dollar bill and my card.
'We'll see,' he said and closed the door firmly in my face.
The harsh realities of Kings Cross were a shock after the gilded gloom of Ridge's. The usual drunken bands of westies roamed the streets looking for somewhere novel to throw up, and the usual prostitutes nodded out in doorways. The place stank like a carnival.
I elbowed my way through the strollers and gapers to Fitzroy Gardens, beat some dithering tourists to the last table in an outdoor coffee shop and watched the denizens gearing up for the

night's commerce. Ancient, tattooed fifteen year olds painted over the bruises and struggled into spiked heels; watched by a bored crowd, a few black drunks staged a shouting and shoving match; giggly Japanese tourists photographed each other against a backdrop of round-eyed riff-raff and the downtown yuppies started to trickle in for pre-dinner drinks in the expensive Macleay Street bistros.

Over coffee and Black Forest cake I wondered what I'd got myself into. Luther was right. It did seem far fetched that a woman like Margaret Cromer would hang out at Ronny Brackenridge's dive, but her husband had received an anonymous phone call, and some money was missing from their joint account. She'd been gone two days now, so he was checking out the options before calling in the police and risking the hot breath of the afternoon papers on his neck.

New Right politicians can't afford to advertise missing wives with criminal connections. I was doing damage control. As Barry Cromer's press secretary, I was no stranger to sleaze.

When Luther Huck called, I was at home watching television, drinking beer and finishing off last night's ham and pineapple pizza.

'She's here,' he said.
'What's she doing?'
'Having dinner with Ronny.' He sounded as amazed as I was.
'With Ronny Brackenridge?'

I was boring him. 'Bring my other fifty dollars, Fish,' said the gracious Huck, slamming down the phone in my ear.

I put my suit coat back on, decided nobody at Ridge's would be offended by my eleven o'clock shadow, and set off for the Cross. I left a message on Cromer's answering machine saying where I was going. I wasn't exactly expecting to get kidnapped and bumped off, but people have been known to have accidents at the Cross.

Huck let me in and my money disappeared into his enormous paw faster than an ace up a card sharp's sleeve. I'd probably never be able to to squeeze it out of Cromer, who still had the first pound note he'd been bribed with. The doorman pointed to a banquette in the corner, and sure enough, there was Margaret Cromer dining with Ronny Brackenridge of the Jaguar with the RONNY plates and the Pet of the Year girlfriends and a very broad range of acquaintances in politics, the racing fraternity and some of the meaner streets of South East Asia.

It was Cromer's wife, all right, but not the tamped down Mosman matron in the photograph. The frills and pearls had gone; this woman was all teeth and tits, and Ronny was in imminent danger of falling down her cleavage.

They made a delightful couple, tanned and sparkling, with the look of health that comes from clean living or hours in expensive gyms with sunlamps and society masseurs. I thought her taste stank but Ronny had a certain appeal for certain women. He was vulgar and probably too good looking, but he had the sly verve of a snake oil salesman and the nerves of a futures trader. I could see how Margaret Cromer wouldn't be burning to leap back into bed with Fat Barry.

What I couldn't figure out was how she'd met Brackenridge.

I lurked near the bar wondering what the hell I was supposed to do — bust up the party and frogmarch her back to the North Shore, or try to reach Cromer and let him stage his own abduction. While I drank the most expensive beer in the southern hemisphere, the problem was solved. A photographer swam into view, an ageing blonde with the hopeless look of a woman who has to keep smiling but can't remember why. She smiled hard at Brackenridge, who beckoned her over.

And there it was, in glorious polaroid for posterity: Margaret Cromer, wife of leading wowser politician, tête-à-tête with notorious vice figure in a Kings Cross gambling den (I was already thinking in headlines). They laughed over the photo and Ronny placed it carefully in his jacket pocket.

I exited left, fought my way through the thickening crowd of revellers, fortune tellers, hookers, buskers, drifters and grafters and their victims, innocent or otherwise, and went home. Tomorrow would be soon enough to tell Cromer. I had lost my appetite for pizza.

Fortified with three cups of coffee and a chocolate donut, I went into Cromer's office next morning and told him I'd found his wife.

'Where is the bitch?' he screamed, practically leaping over the desk — no mean feat for a fifty-year old, hundred kilo politician with high blood pressure and a shrunken liver.

'At this moment I'm not absolutely certain,' I hedged, taking up a defensive position behind a leather armchair. 'But last night she dined at Ridge's as a personal guest of the proprietor.' (And was probably still in bed with him.)

'Brackenridge!' howled Cromer. 'That smarmy bastard!' As an afterthought, he bellowed: 'Brackenridge, my arse! It's obvious he's a wog of some sort!'

'Please,' I begged. 'Not even in jest. Remember the ethnic vote.'

He was beginning to rant. 'There's more,' I interrupted: 'Pictures.' I told him what had happened.

'Go and see Brackenridge,' he ordered. 'Find out what the fuck is going on. That bitch is up to something.'

'Wouldn't you rather handle it yourself?' I pleaded. 'I mean, it's a very personal thing...'

'The bastard's taking photographs,' he snarled. 'Do you want a picture of me and Brackenridge in the *Sun Herald*? It's your job to keep me out of the bloody papers.'

I loitered.

'If you don't do it, I'll get Farquarson,' he threatened. He had me. There was no way I was giving an opening to Farquarson, his private secretary, a young man with mysterious links with Right to Life, the Queensland National Party, a CIA-funded think tank and half the SP bookies in Sydney. Farquarson was ambitious and possessed the confidence of a teenage porn tycoon. Anyone with a soul hated him on sight: he was bound to succeed.

He was hanging round the door when I came out. 'What's happening?'

'Nothing.'

'The old boy is so nervous he's shedding skins,' he said, scoring a direct hit on the psoriasis that soured Cromer's disposition and made his image engineers despair.

'You're so charming, Farquarson,' I said. 'Do us all a favour and join the Labor Party.'

I escaped before he could subject me to more socratic questioning and called Luther Huck and told him to set up a meet with Brackenridge. Meantime I hit the Wentworth and drank too many Victoria Bitters and discussed politics and horses with Betty. As

Betty was a keen student of human nature, like all barmaids, I showed her the picture of Margaret Cromer.

'Not a happy lady,' she remarked. 'Who is she?'

'The boss's wife.'

Enough said: she snorted and moved off down the bar to serve a loud-mouthed barrister.

What we had both seen in Margaret Cromer's eyes was desperation. Knowing Barry as I did, I fully understood why she'd bolted: what I couldn't understand was why I was helping him get her back. Several more beers numbed my conscience sufficiently to front Luther Huck at Ridge's. He smelt of grog and aggro and let me in without a word.

Brackenridge was waiting for me wearing a Zegna suit and more aftershave than a Mexican airline steward. We shook hands — a manicure, too. Ronny must have decided I needed solid food, for he called over a waiter with a patronising sneer and dirty fingernails.

'Calimari and chips,' I said. 'And a Heineken.'

'Jesus, Syd, you've got no taste at all,' said Ronny. 'At least have the lobster.'

The waiter, who was enjoying this, fiddled with the cutlery: maybe Ridge's gave you fish knives with your calamari. 'Piss off,' I said finally, and he flounced away.

'Was that absolutely necessary?' asked Ronny.

'I don't like dirty fingernails,' I said.

Ronny's smile faded and I had a vision of him personally removing the offending fingernails with a pair of pliers. 'OK, Ronny,' I led. 'What's the deal?'

'A hundred grand for the picture,' he said, laying it gently on the table like a winning poker hand.

I was momentarily winded. 'He'll never pay it. He's tighter than a budgie's bum.'

Ronny laughed. It wasn't only the money he wanted: Cromer was a great anti-gambling crusader and an even greater hypocrite. 'How's the old boy taking it?'

'Not all that well,' I replied. 'He suggested you were a wog on the make.' I had nothing to lose, by this time I detested everyone involved in the transaction, myself included.

Ronnie's synthetic bonhomie evaporated, giving me a sneak

preview of how he'd look in ten years' time, when the means had begun to show through the ends. Two new sharp lines bracketed his mouth, which wasn't smiling.

'At least I don't beat my wife,' he said, which I found slightly sophistic, given that he wasn't in the habit of marrying the bimbos he beat up.

And that's when it clicked: I took out my photo and placed it beside Brackenridge's. The look on Margaret Cromer's face was fear; the woman I'd seen in the club had never been afraid of a man in her life. I grinned at Brackenridge: 'It's a better job than Fine Cotton, Ronny, but it's still a ring-in. Who is she?'

He hesitated, then said: 'I'll get her.' It was too easy: he hadn't played his last card yet.

Summoning the waiter, who was sulking behind the bar, he said: 'Ask Miss Kincaid to come in, would you Mark? And clean those fucking fingernails.'

She exploded into the room in a red silk dress that knew exactly where to touch down, shook my hand and said: 'I'm Katy Kincaid, Margaret's twin sister.' Then she touched Ronny's arm gently and murmured: 'Thank you, Ronny darling. I can probably manage now.'

Ronny beamed at her, gave me a hard-man look and left. The waiter arrived with my calamari and clean fingernails. He glared at me and beamed at Katy Kincaid. I was beaming too: I was in love. She was even better close up—black hair, light tan, and pale blue eyes the colour of the most expensive diamonds. Margaret Cromer had the same features: it was the packaging that made the difference.

'What's the perfume?' I asked.

'Money,' she said, and we laughed.

She quickly got down to business. 'I've taken some trouble to set this up, Mr Fish...'

'Syd,' I interrupted.

'OK, Syd. And you've buggered it up. But I want you to know why I did it.'

She was very persuasive but then I'm easily led, especially by beautiful women. All she wanted, she said, was some repayment for all the years of humiliation her sister had endured at the pudgy hands of my employer. Something to help Margaret Cromer forget.

'A hundred grand buys a lot of amnesia,' I remarked.

'Regard it as accident compensation,' she said. 'Loss of earnings, pain and suffering. Marg is a casualty. She's unemployable.'

'What does she think about all this?'

'She doesn't know. She's hiding in my apartment at the Gold Coast having a nervous breakdown. She thinks I'm away on a business trip.'

'Which you are.'

'Which I am,' she agreed. 'Marg took some money out of an account and she's terrified Fatso will come after her and beat her up.'

'I'm sure he'll give it careful consideration,' I said.

'I've got friends, too,' she said, and smiled.

'She could always take him to court,' I suggested, fighting a rearguard action.

'Cromer would buy a QC and wipe the floor with my sister,' said Katy Kincaid. 'And Marg would give in without a fight. She's a lady, you see, and ladies lose.'

I liked her. She was tough and funny, and could have put Channel 10 into profit in twelve months. Whatever her game, I was on her team. All that remained was to get the ball past Barry, and it looked as if I'd be carrying it.

'But how come Cromer didn't spring you?' I asked. He must know his wife's got a twin sister.'

'If he'd twigged,' she said reasonably, 'the cops would have been crawling all over me in ten seconds.' She told me she'd been overseas doing the grand tour when her sister had married Cromer, and he couldn't get his new wife away from the Kincaids fast enough. 'Cromer didn't want Marg's bog Irish family hanging around with their hands out,' she said. 'I've never actually met the man.'

It sounded like the Cromer I knew.

'And haven't you noticed how people who cheat all the time are really gullible themselves?' she marvelled.

Like me, I thought.

There was just one other small worm of doubt: 'Where does

Ronny Brackenridge fit into all this?'

'Ah,' she said. She'd been waiting for this. 'Ronny and I are old friends. We went to the same high school and I ran into him again at university.'

I choked: she laughed. 'Ronny financed his BA with gambling. Mostly playing poker with the Asian students. And winning, I might add.' Cheating, I thought. 'I think he had a racehorse, too.'

'A BA,' I croaked. 'Ronny Brackenridge, BA. The bastard can't read or write.'

'He didn't have to. I did all his English assignments.' She was enjoying herself. 'I used to make him write them out in his own handwriting and put some spelling mistakes in. For authenticity.'

'How did he do?' I asked.

'Mostly credits, I didn't think they'd believe distinctions.'

The look on my face made her think I was shocked. In fact I was just jealous: I'd failed English.

'Don't knock it,' she said. 'Ronny paid very well. It beat the hell out of waitressing.'

She went on: 'You could say Ronny was a formative influence. I thought about him a lot while I was teaching primary school in the western suburbs and living in a cockroach farm at Kirribilli.'

'A lot of people are worse off.'

'It's all relative,' she answered.

'Yeah. Anyway, I don't picture you as a school teacher.'

'Exactly. I hit Ronny for a loan and took off for the Gold Coast.' She'd met lots of men on the Gold Coast, men who knew how money worked and loved to talk about it, and she'd listened hard.

'They weren't interested in my opinions. It didn't occur to them I had a brain.'

'How unsporting of them.'

She laughed: 'Look, I'm not whingeing, Syd. I got an education. All they got was a quick feel.'

She'd used her brain to turn all that information into a couple of dress shops and some flats. 'So I've always had a soft spot for Ronny.'

'OK, I'm in,' I said. 'I'll give it a go.'

'Good.' She dug into a little gold purse and produced several pictures of herself and Ronny Brackenridge in highly compromising positions. 'You might need these.'

'You photograph well,' I said.

She put her arms around my neck and kissed me. 'Sometimes you need a snake to catch a toad,' she whispered. When I calmed down several hours later, I wondered what that made me.

To make a long story short, I took the photos back to Cromer, weathered the abuse and hysteria, watched fear and greed battle it out and fear win, and couriered the cash back to Ridge's. All in a day's work. Katy Kincaid stacked the money neatly in a leather briefcase, thanked me and said I'd always be welcome at the Gold Coast. With all the other conmen, fugitives and losers in search of some sunshine and a ray of hope, I thought.

Cromer never did find out exactly what had happened, but with the unerring instincts of a sewer rat, he knew I was in it up to my armpits. So it wasn't long before I got the summons.

He was sprawled behind his huge cedar power desk in his leather executive power chair, with his fat arms clasped behind his head, exuding a degree of arrogance exclusive to political hacks, bankers, property developers and successful heroin importers.

'The trouble with you,' he began, even before I'd sat down, 'Is that you're arrogant.' He stabbed a beefy finger in my general direction: 'But you're not nearly as smart as you think you are.'

'What's the problem?' I asked.

'I don't want any smartarses on my staff. You can't get along with the others — Farquarson? — and you're not getting me enough good press. You're fired.'

I got up. 'Haven't you got anything to say for yourself?' he asked, disappointed.

'Yeah,' I said. 'I do, actually. Barry, do you still beat your wife?'

That night I sat down with a large scotch and considered my options. My list of saleable skills was alarmingly short, most of my experience was as a snoop or a fixer. As I now stank like last Friday's prawn heads with both political parties and their best mates' newspapers, my options were limited.

Dispirited, I turned on the TV and got the eighth re-run of

Cannon. Watching William Conrad puffing around after wrongdoers half his age, I decided I could act as well and run faster: perhaps I had a future after all.

I picked up the phone and called an old school friend. When he could drag himself away from running the Labor Party's gossip machine, Dave Mitchell did media relations for the police, so I figured he'd have the information I wanted. He also had a good sense of humour: when I asked him what you had to do to get a private investigator's licence, I thought he'd never stop laughing.

HEAVEN SENT

He came into my Darlinghurst office wearing a stupid grin and a brown suit, neither of which seemed to fit.

'Billy Cleat,' he said, offering a hand the size of a Christmas ham. The name conjured up thousands of manhours lost in front of suburban TV sets on Saturday afternoons. Billy Cleat was a Rugby League legend gone to fat and more recently to hell, and now it looked as if he were my client.

Someday I'll meet one of my heroes before he hits bottom.

'Luther Huck told me you find people,' he said. 'Luther's a friend of mine.'

I was mildly surprised. I found it hard to believe Luther Huck had friends. Or even a mother, for that matter.

Billy Cleat's unmelodious voice dragged me back from an erotic reverie about Katy Kincaid. 'I want you to find Devon.'

'What? Where?' I asked.

'It's a her,' he said patiently. 'My lady, Devon Kent.'

A narrow escape. You don't make mistakes with brain-dead brunos like Billy Cleat, they might get irritable and kick a goal with your head.

He told me about it. Billy was chauffeuring for Larry Azzarro, a drug boss who'd made guest appearances in at least two Royal Commissions to my knowledge. Azzarro was slick and vicious and operated out of a well-fortified Italianate mansion in Bellevue Hill. Devon Kent was one of Larry's hand-me-downs, and she'd gone missing. Privately I thought she must have been getting rather frayed around the edges to take on Billy Cleat.

Billy didn't tell the story quite like that, of course, he was in love.

'What's Devon do?' I asked. 'Where does she hang out?'

'She's an exotic dancer. But I don't think she's been working much lately.'

That meant another source of income — hooking or dealing or both.

'Why not?' I asked innocently.

'She's been sick,' he said. Smack.

'So when did you see her last?'

'A coupla weeks ago. She was up at the house.'

'Azzarro's house?' Were they still friends, or just business associates? 'What for?'

He hesitated. 'They keep in touch.'

He wasn't telling me much: he didn't want me to get the right idea about his girlfriend.

'Why do you think something happened to her, Billy? Hasn't she ever dropped out of sight before?'

'Yeah, but she wouldn't now. I mean, I uh... was getting something for her. She said she'd come and pick it up.'

I had to ask. 'Drugs?' I hoped he wouldn't take offence and drop-kick me to the moon.

'Shit, no,' he said, shocked. Billy had a strange sort of innocence, or maybe it was just too many knocks on the head.

'Well?'

Finally he squeezed it out. 'Money.'

It was serious. Ladies like Devon Kent might miss their mother's funeral, a court appearance, or even the entire Bicentenary, but they always turned up for drugs or money.

'So she dropped in on you, visited your boss, then went up in smoke. Have you asked Larry about it?'

'Yeah, he says she left around midnight and he hasn't heard from her since.'

'And you believe that?'

He gaped at me. 'I suppose I do, yeah.'

'But you didn't see her leave?'

'Nah, I sleep out the back with the cars. I can't see people going in and out.'

Of course not. I had a sudden flash of Billy's life — *Boys Own* hero reduced to a room over the garage, a colour TV and Larry

Azzarro's cast-off tarts. It made my life look glamorous.

'Did Larry go out that night?'

'If he did, I didn't drive him.'

'Could he have taken the car without you knowing?'

'He can't drive,' said Billy.

So however she left the house, it hadn't been in the boot of one of Larry's Mercedes. She might have left in a taxi. Or on the 368 bus. Or maybe she hitched a ride to Queensland to start a new life. Maybe.

I made one last stab at dragging something useful out of him. 'Tell me about Devon, Billy. Who does she owe? Who are her friends? Who'd want her out of the way?'

He seemed helpless. 'She knows everybody, Syd.'

'Give me somewhere to start, mate,' I pleaded.

He racked his brains, which didn't take long, and told me Devon shared a flat in Elizabeth Bay with Grace Ho. I asked him for the phone number.

He avoided my eye. 'Ah, I don't know. Devon always called me.'

From the way that depressed me, I could tell I was beginning to like the poor dumb bastard. I was also picking up Devon's spoor, and she smelled like a user. Lots of people might have wanted her out of their lives.

As I was seeing him out, he said: 'Be heaven sent with Devon Kent.'

'What?!'

He repeated it. 'That's how they used to advertise Devon's act,' he explained slowly, as if I were an idiot. It would stick to my brain like a burr.

I promised to get back to him and he shambled off, a gentleman to the last, protecting a lady's name. The Christian Brothers would have been proud of him.

If Devon's friends weren't talking, I'd have to sniff out some of her enemies. By that time she'd probably have turned up from a weekend at the Gold Coast with a Japanese businessman, a long binge in a filthy flat somewhere in Bondi, or a short sojourn in a psych ward.

After a couple of sausage rolls and a Coke, I called my best friend, Lizzie Darcy. Lizzie is a journalist who lives on gossip and knows all the bit players in the Sydney milieu — their records, aliases, feuds, and even their poor little old mothers down in The Rocks. We arranged to meet that night in the Great Western on Broadway.

I thought about Lizzie while I sat waiting in the pub, eating stale peanuts and listening to a couple of sub-editors moaning about cadets (some things never change). Lizzie was small, dark and intense, with an evil laugh and a mind like a laser. She wasn't beautiful but she had a force field that lit up a room. I lusted after her intermittently, but she'd long ago turned me into a friend, and when I finally recovered my punctured pride I was glad because so far I'd outlasted all the lovers.

'Tell me about Devon Kent,' I said, after we'd organised some beers.

'She's a hooker and a junkie and she's got a big mouth,' said Lizzie. 'That's the short answer.'

I was liking this case less and less. Lizzie told me Devon had worked her way up from stripping, through dealing drugs, to Azzarro's constant companionship before her habit took over. When Azzarro kicked her out she started talking too much — to the newspapers, some said to the police. There were even rumours she was having it off with a narc, whose name Lizzie supplied. People were getting very nervous. Devon was dealing again, and there was talk she owed big money. Billy was right, a cast of thousands.

'You seem to know a lot about her,' I said.

'I did a series on personalities of the Cross and interviewed Devon,' Lizzie snapped. 'Don't you read the paper anymore?'

I realised I had seen it, but at the time Devon had been just another relentless self-promoter. 'She must have something going for her if a big harmless dope like Cleat is in love with her,' I said quickly, to deflect Lizzie's fire.

'Billy's in love with some role Devon plays for clapped-out footballers who'll lend her money, put up with her bullshit and frighten the other goons off. She's manipulative and very street smart. And she looks pretty good for someone who's been on the game on and off for fifteen years.'

She surveyed herself sourly in the grimy pub mirror: 'I don't know how they do it.'

I told her she would always be beautiful to me, but she wasn't listening. 'To be fair, there was something special about Devon,' she said. 'Till the smack took over she used to be very glamorous in a sleazy sort of way. Very dashing. But lately she's just very... very, if you know what I mean.'

We drank on in glum silence. 'What about Grace Ho, Liz?' I asked, remembering what I'd come for.

'Amazing Grace? Is Devon still living with her? Grace should have kicked her out ages ago.'

She told me Grace was a model who'd got sick of having to starve herself and screw photographers to make a living and had moved into couriering drugs from Thailand.

'Is she still in the business?'

'I imagine so,' said Lizzie. 'It would be hard to give up that sort of money. But she certainly isn't a mule anymore. What with equal opportunity and all, she'd be a senior executive with one of the Chinese syndicates by now.'

'Why the nickname?'

'Amazing Grace?' She smirked: 'You'll find out soon enough.'

'Give me a break. What's she like?'

Lizzie pondered, then grinned at me. 'Grace Ho is very... Chinese.'

I had to confess I hadn't been able to get hold of Grace's phone number. Shaking her head at my incompetence, Lizzie looked it up in her battered contact book.

As we got up to leave, she said: 'Devon's either gone underground for her own good, or been put there for someone else's. I'd put my money on the latter.' She smiled gently: 'The latter means the last one.'

I went off in a huff, her nasty laugh like bullets in my back.

'You'll love the apartment,' she called.

Amazing Grace wasn't at all interested in seeing me till I said: 'Lizzie Darcy thinks Devon Kent is probably in the Harbour without her water wings.'

We arranged to meet.

I'm not sure what I had expected a Chinese drug queen to look like, but Grace Ho was straight out of *Vogue*. The French edition.

'Are you buying, Mr Fish, or just looking?' she chirruped.

She was tall for a Chinese, and as highly polished as very good jade. Clothes, Double Bay; eyes rounded off to the nearest $5000.

The apartment was neo-Deco, with high ceilings, parquetry floors, a glassed-in conservatory with a jungle and real birds, and views to the Heads. Very stylish, and not what you would automatically associate with Devon Kent, stripper and junkie.

'Nice apartment,' I remarked.

'Thank you, Mr Fish. It has already doubled in value. And I own three others in this building.'

I could have sworn I heard the click of an abacus. 'Do you collect shoes, too?' I asked, po faced.

She frowned. 'Ah, a little joke.'

She made tea and watched expressionlessly while I put milk and sugar in mine. 'Perhaps you would also like a fortune cookie, Mr Fish?'

It was hard to concentrate, up to my neck in a silky leather couch and wraparound Harbour views, but I was able to ascertain that Grace hadn't been particularly worried about Devon, who often disappeared for weeks at a time.

'Are you sure she wasn't in trouble?' I asked.

'There is always danger in the streets, Mr Fish,' said Grace, sipping tea, impenetrable as the I Ching.

'Did she have any enemies?'

Devon knew so many people, Grace said. It was just possible some of them did not care for her. Grace Ho wasn't giving anything away. I was surprised she wasn't charging me by the minute for the view.

'So you've got no ideas?'

She smiled without warmth: 'There is no future in ideas, Mr Fish. Especially big ideas.' Dropping her eyes, she retreated into the overacted inscrutability I'd last seen on Anna May Wong in *Shanghai Express*. But she did tell me she hadn't seen Devon since the night she'd visited Azzarro.

'What was she wearing?'

Grace led me to her friend's bedroom. Devon was closer here: it was all frills, spilt makeup and photos of Devon in varying degrees of undress. The girl's energy and recklessness leapt out of the pictures. She was small, blond and curvy, not really beautiful — her blue eyes protruded slightly, and there was a gap between her front teeth — but the little defects made her look vulnerable. She became real for me for the first time, and I began to hope she wasn't dead.

Grace opened an enormous walk-in wardrobe. Now, I don't know much about clothes but even to me Devon's looked gaudy. She was as overdressed as an opera singer. Certainly Amazing Grace wouldn't be caught dead in any of this gear.

She riffled through the racks and said: 'Red leather skirt, red silk shirt.'

I decided I was being conned: 'Shoes?'

Grace looked down. 'Red, of course.' She smiled in triumph: 'Snake-skin sling backs, high-heeled.'

Catching the look on my face, she added: 'Devon's shoes were always the same colour as her dress, Mr Fish. She was, I think you would call it, a monochromaniac?'

That too, I thought.

Grace raised an eyebrow and pointed to the fifty or more pairs of shoes. 'As you can see, it was Devon who collected shoes, Mr Fish.' Game, set, match, Grace Ho.

I noticed, however, that Grace had started using the past tense about Devon Kent.

Vanquished, I was shown the door. I felt as if I'd been beaten to a pulp with a paper fan. But I was still curious. 'Tell me, Ms Ho, exactly where did Devon Kent fit into your scheme of things?'

Grace was beginning to realise Devon was probably dead, murdered most likely, and the mask slipped a millimetre. 'Devon was my friend, Mr Fish. How can I explain, except to say she was very...' Her hands fluttered as she tried to convey Devon's essence. 'Very alive.'

And now, I thought, probably very dead. Our eyes met. The door closed gently in my face.

I might have felt sorry for Grace if I hadn't felt sorrier for the bundles of rags lying in Kings Cross alleyways dying for her merchandise. They probably had friends somewhere too.

My next move was to call Dave Mitchell at Police HQ: I needed to know where Devon's policeman was when she disappeared. Dave wasn't all that keen till I asked him if his Minister knew who'd started the rumours about his wife's distinctions in her criminology course at Sydney University. In the last version I'd heard the politician's principal private secretary had written most of the assignments.

That night I wrung Azzarro's unlisted number out of Billy, and fortified by several beers, rang the house. A surly minder answered, I said I wanted to talk to his boss and he asked why. I was trying to find Devon Kent, I explained.

'What do you think this is, shithead?' he screamed, 'A fucking travel agency?' and hung up. I started getting nostalgic for my old job with Barry Cromer. I was obviously going soft. Next I'd be sentimentalising my stint on the Melbourne *Truth*.

To comfort myself, I went to one of the last real cafes, near Central, and ate fish in thick yellow batter, chips, frozen peas, several slices of white bread, apple pie and ice cream and a pot of stewed tea.

There were two messages on my machine when I got home — Billy wanting to know if I had any news, and the soft staccato voice of Grace Ho: 'I wondered, Mr Fish, if you knew Angel Gloria was at the house the night Devon went missing.' I kept calling Grace's number, but got only a recorded brush-off.

Who the hell was Angel Gloria?

One person in Sydney was sure to know. Lizzie was still at work and didn't want to be bothered.

'Piss off, Syd,' Lizzie answered. 'I'm waiting for a call.'

Lizzie was having a bumpy affair with a devious political apparatchik who lived on planes and thought every Labor government in the country would fall if he took an hour off.

'From Machiavelli?'

'Do I need this?' she asked through clenched teeth.

'Just tell me who Angel Gloria is,' I pleaded.

'Meet me at Coluzzi's at ten o'clock tomorrow morning.'

My phone rang, very late. A husky female voice that had laughed and smoked and boozed through thousands of nights said: 'I hear you're looking for Devon Kent.'

I didn't know whose side she was on, so I was noncommittal.

'Everybody knows,' she said. 'Just like they know you're not going to find her. Alive, that is.'

'How do they know?'

'Devon burned Larry Azzarro for ten thousand bucks a couple of weeks ago. She was calling in a lot of old debts before she disappeared. Or trying to.'

'Did she raise the money?'

'No. People were getting pretty sick of Devon toward the end. She ran out of credit.'

'What's your interest?' I asked.

'I loved Devon,' she replied simply. 'Larry Azzarro killed her, and I want somebody to nail the bastard.'

I seriously doubted it would be me, but I thanked her and sat staring at the phone, wondering how many of my friends would be around if I needed ten thousand dollars urgently.

Coluzzi's coffee shop was crowded, deafening and full of arty-looking yuppies hoping for a glimpse of Brett Whiteley, so we sat outside. We had to fight it out with the flies but at least it was cooler.

'Angel Gloria,' I prompted.

'Tell me what you know first.'

'Grace Ho tipped me off. Said Angel Gloria was at Azzarro's house that night.

'Ah,' said Lizzie, nodding to herself, while I mainlined caffeine and cherry Danish. 'What did you think of Grace, by the way?'

'You were right,' I said, watching her eyebrows and expectations rise — she was dying to hear how Grace had mauled me — 'I liked the apartment.'

'God, you never change, do you?' she said, narrowing her eyes, but relented and told me that the Angel had replaced Devon in Azzarro's affections, which was one way of putting it. Lizzie described her as a Devon clone — tiny, exquisite, blond, blue-eyed. The Angel called herself a model, though she tended to do most of her posing without the inconvenience of clothes.

Lizzie was entranced by Gloria. 'Here's this incredible looking woman who's a complete primitive, a social leper. She doesn't know the difference between right and wrong — lies, cheats, whores around, pinches anything that's not nailed down. She's learned to keep her mouth shut most of the time but if something sets her off, she's utterly vile.' Lizzie laughed: 'A real dirty little girl, that one.'

'Drugs?'

'I don't think so. She's so stupid, she's sort of naturally spaced out.'

Gloria's background explained a lot: second-generation welfare family, father an alcoholic recidivist who loved his daughters a little too much, mother ten IQ points off retarded. It was a miracle the Angel got out at all, Lizzie thought.

'Only as far as Azzarro's bedroom,' I commented.

'Give credit where it's due,' Lizzie scolded. 'At least the bedroom is in Bellevue Hill. She could be propping up a door in Darlinghurst Road.'

'If Gloria knows something, I'll have to worm it out of her without Azzarro knowing, or he'll rip my arms off,' I said. 'How the hell am I going to do that?'

I didn't get any sympathy. 'Gloria works out at the Oxford Gym every day,' said Lizzie, looking at her watch. 'If you hurry, you'll catch her.'

The Oxford Gym was full of gays working on their immune systems, housewives working on their cellulite, and a sprinkling of models and dancers gaining through pain. It didn't take me long to locate Angel Gloria, succulent in the faintest suggestion of a silver gym suit. I could see why she chose the Oxford Gym: if she'd popped her pectorals downtown at the Hyde Park, she would have caused more coronaries than the crash of '87.

I changed into my shorts and ageing running shoes and surveyed myself in the mirror. A mistake. After briefly contemplating suicide or a month at a fat farm, I pulled myself together and sidled up to the Angel, who was puffing away on the Nautilus.

I introduced myself. The vacant blue eyes sucked me in and spat me out. Insulting but understandable.

'I'm a friend of Grace Ho's,' I persisted. 'She told me I should talk to you.'

Amazing Grace's name catapulted Gloria into the fight or flight mode. 'Who the fuck are you, and what do you want?' The voice had an edge like a buzz saw.

'I'm looking for Devon Kent,' I said. 'Her friend, Mr Cleat, seems to think she may have met with a misadventure.' I can be mean too.

Her jaw dropped: 'What?'

I translated. 'Devon Kent has disappeared and Grace Ho thinks you know something about it.'

'I don't know any Devon Kent,' she said, her voice rising.

'But you were at the house when she came to see Larry, weren't you?'

'No. I've never met her. I don't know nothing!' Her cherubic face had clanged shut and the blue eyes were frightened. She wasn't all that pretty now.

I hammered away, 'How did Devon get back to town that night? Did Larry call her a cab?'

'No. I don't know. I told you I wasn't there!' she shrieked. 'Fuck off! Leave me alone!'

Roused by the rumpus, a gorilla in a powder blue track suit padded over and escorted me firmly to the door. I went quietly. Behind me, red-faced and furious, the Angel spat obscenities.

As I massaged my bruised biceps, I wondered when Larry Azzarro would realise that his fetish for small dangerous blondes was costing too much. I had an uncomfortable feeling he'd be paying me a visit soon, so I threw some gear into my trusty old black Valiant and checked into a cheap motel.

Back in my office later that day, Lizzie's disembodied voice informed me that Devon had been found in the bush beside the F6. She sounded upset. When I called back I found out why— Devon had been beaten to death. With fists.

'What was she wearing?' I asked.

Lizzie consulted the report. 'Red silk blouse, red leather miniskirt.'

'And red shoes?' I asked.

'Doesn't say anything about shoes.' She went away to talk to the police roundsman. 'Dennis says there were no shoes at the scene. She must have lost them in the fight or in the car. They're probably in a creek by now, or at the tip. Is it important?'

'No, I was just trying to score a point.'

Lizzie laughed. 'I warned you about Grace Ho, didn't I?'

Somebody should have warned me about Lizzie Darcy: she can read my mind.

'Thanks,' I said. 'Now all I have to do is tell Billy before he hears it on the Macquarie News.'

As I'm basically a moral coward, I decided to do it over the phone. It didn't work. Billy told me to meet him at the Dolphin in Crown Street.

When we found a quiet table in the beer garden, I told Billy everything I knew, down to the missing red shoes.

'Devon has... had this thing about shoes,' said Billy morosely.

I wanted to keep it businesslike. 'Looks like I'm off the case now, Billy. The cops will be all over it now.'

He wasn't paying attention. 'I heard you been talking to Gloria.'

'Yeah, if you could call it that.' After I'd related the incident in the gym I asked: 'Was Gloria there that night, Billy? Grace thinks she was.'

'Grace said that?' He was impressed: Grace Ho's opinions carried a lot of freight on this turf. 'She probably was there, Syd. She usually is.'

'Billy, how did Devon get out to the Wollongong road from Bellevue Hill? You didn't take her, and Larry can't drive.'

There was a long silence, and finally something connected in the back of Billy's brain. It was like watching a light go on in an empty warehouse.

'Gloria's got a car,' he said.

'But you told me nobody took the cars out.'

'Gloria's car doesn't fit in the garage. She parks it in the lane beside the house.'

'There's a lane? Can you see it from your room?'

'No.'

'Could Gloria have taken the car out without being seen?'

'There's a gate,' he said. Just like that: 'There's a gate.'

'Where's the car now, Billy?'

'It got stolen.' His voice was flat. Suddenly he looked old. Hope had fled, along with the years, the muscle tone and the adulation. He sat on in silence for a while, absently drinking, thinking of Devon perhaps. Then he paid his bill in cash, shook my hand, thanked me graciously and left.

I closed up my office and went out and got drunk, had dinner with a sympathetic lady lawyer, and danced my arse off at some disco that I'd never be able to find again, drank more, went back home and passed out. The next morning found me wounded, but not as badly as Billy Cleat, I feared.

I rang Lizzie and cried on her shoulder till she got sick of me. 'Jesus, Syd, everybody's got problems. They're about to lay off half the staff here and my boyfriend's got the whole goddamm Labor Party gunning for him. At least you've only got Larry Azzarro to worry about.'

'Thanks, cobber,' I said and rang off.

A week later Dave Mitchell rang and told me Devon's policeman had been in Griffith the weekend she disappeared.

Time passes. I'd regained my equilibrium when Lizzie called in the early hours of a Sunday morning to tell me that Billy Cleat, Larry Azzarro and Angel Gloria were dead: Billy had lost control of the Jag coming out of the Kings Cross tunnel and smashed head-on into a pylon.

'What do you think, Syd?' asked Lizzie, subdued.

'Would Billy Cleat lose control of a car? Just now, just like that?'

'It could happen. He hits the piss.'

'But if he did it on purpose, he must have decided they killed Devon. Maybe he found some proof.'

If he did, we would never know. The case was closed.

The Glebe Morgue is old, cold and eerie, and smells of chemicals and mortality. The mortuary attendant moves swiftly and skilfully about his tasks.

Inured as he is to sudden and violent death, he pauses for a moment to mourn the perfection of Gloria's naked body, which seems to glow in the gloom. No one would want to look at her face now, though.

He sighs and gets on with it, labelling her personal effects and sealing them in plastic bags. He doesn't look twice at the elegant high-heeled red shoes which add an almost obscene splash of colour to Angel Gloria's last gig.

THE PORNOGRAPHER'S SON

Although it probably said Investor on his tax return, those with their ears to the gutter called Bernie Coogan a pornographer.

I thought of this when he rang one morning and asked me to come to Coogee to see him.

'What for?' I asked. I don't like Coogan, whom I'd met a few times through my ex-boss Barry Cromer, who was now making a complete ass of himself as Minister for Criminal Justice.

Coogan was self made, and he'd done a lousy job of it. His personality was as unsavoury as his career, which had started in tow trucks and slithered its way up through a chain of smash repair shops. But so far nobody had managed to pin anything actionable on him.

'It's bloody important, Fish,' he said. 'I can't talk about it on the phone.'

I could understand that in New South Wales: God knows how many crime-busters, journalists, hackers and handicapped activists were listening in and recording the conversation. It was enough to turn any self-respecting hood into a civil libertarian.

As I didn't particularly want to get mixed up with Coogan, I hesitated.

'It's a personal matter, Syd,' he urged, and his voice wobbled. He had me then. I couldn't resist the opportunity of seeing Coogan down — I wanted to meet whoever was squeezing his balls.

The South Coogee house was a crim's dream, with four or five architectural styles battling it out, columns and arches everywhere, a huge, unused swimming pool and the latest in electronic security.

Patrolling the grounds were several attack dogs which immediately announced my arrival.

After I'd given everything but my mother's maiden name over the intercom, a redhead half Coogan's age ushered me in. The girl had a hesitant, temporary look, stemming perhaps from the fact that she was the third Mrs Coogan and a suspicion that she would not be the last.

She seemed at a loss. 'Hello, I'm Syd Fish,' I prompted, proffering a hand. She shied slightly, as if I were about to hit her or serve her with divorce papers, but rallied and whispered, 'Michele'.

'Your husband wants to see me,' I said. It was like pushing a stalled truck.

She stared at me, then said: 'Please sit down. I'll get him.'

The living room looked as if it had been thrown together by a set designer from a drag show, all crushed velvet and mirrors and impossible antiques, but the views compensated.

Coogan appeared eventually, gut well out, shoulders back, very much the tycoon, but he had bags under his eyes and he wasn't wearing his usual arrogant sneer. What he was wearing was the sort of outfit a colour-blind golfer would choose. He was a big, red-skinned, bearlike customer covered in pale ginger hair that made him glow pink in the sun. And like a bear, he only looked cuddly.

He took me into his study, where he probably studied the form guide and tax avoidance schemes, and gave me a Foster's.

'My kid has been snatched,' he said, dispensing with the foreplay.

'Since when have you had any kids?'

'Since sixteen years ago.'

'This has got to be the best kept secret in New South Wales,' I said. 'What brand is it?'

'It's a boy. Luke.'

'Where have you had Luke stashed for sixteen years?'

'He's been with his mother. She pissed off when he was a baby. He turned up here a couple of Christmases ago. Out of the blue.'

'I somehow get the impression you didn't comb the country for his mother all those years ago.'

He didn't like the trend of the questioning: 'Why should I? I didn't want any kids in the first place, and Denise went to the pack, the hippie slut. Hare Krishna, Nimbin, drugs. She's as mad as a cut snake.'

'So who got the ransom note, Denise?'

'No, they contacted me. Luke's been spending his school holidays with me. He was snatched from here.'

I asked him if he'd told Denise.

'No, and I'm not going to, either. I'm going to get the bloody kid back on my own.'

Lots of bad blood there, still. I wondered how Denise felt about the kid staying with Coogan.

'How much do they think a sixteen-year-old kid is worth, Bernie?'

'Half a million.'

'And is he?'

'Yeah,' he said grudgingly. 'He's a good kid.'

I must have looked skeptical, because he became belligerent: 'Besides, if the word got round that I'd been stung for half a million bucks, I'd be a fucking joke in this town.'

I was relieved. If he'd turned out to be human, I might have been expected to like him. 'So what do you want me to do?'

'Check out Denise's friends. I wouldn't trust that bitch an inch. I'll look after this end of it. And I want you to deliver the money, if it comes to that.'

This was a job where the messenger could easily get killed. Coogan was watching my face. 'There's twenty grand in it Fish, if you have to pick up the kid for me.'

If money talks, twenty grand sings: 'How long have we got?'

'Two days.'

'Just for interest's sake, what will you be doing while I'm delivering the dough?'

'Oh, just watching with some of my friends,' he said casually.

A movement caught my eye and I looked up to find Michele hovering by the door. In profile, she was obviously pregnant. Her face was pale and muddy looking, and she seemed frightened.

'OK,' I said. 'Give me Denise's address and I'll start nosing around.'

'I don't have it.'

'What do you mean you don't have it?'

Coogan got stroppy. 'Look, the bloody kid just turned up here. I haven't discussed it with Denise.'

The kid was a chip of the old block. He obviously had considerable organising abilities; everyone was in on this rort except his mother.

'You do know what her name is, I suppose?'

He told me it had been Dwyer, the same as Luke's, but she'd remarried. Knowing there would be hundreds of Dwyers in the phone book, I asked if she had relatives in Sydney.

'God knows,' he said. 'I picked her up in a topless bar. She never talked about her family. I got the impression she'd had a pretty rough time.'

I took a look at Luke's room, but it was carefully anonymous. Bernie didn't have a photo of the boy, but he told me Luke was fair-haired and good-looking, with blue eyes; he looked like Denise when she was young.

'Where did they take him from, Bernie?'

'The beach, I think. I haven't found anyone who saw it happen. Michele took the call, though. Talk to her.'

Michele wasn't very helpful. Luke had gone to the beach on his bike as usual, and hadn't come back. The caller was a man with an Australian accent; she couldn't tell his age. He told her they had two days to get the money, then he'd ring back with instructions. If the cops were called in, they'd dump Luke off the Heads in cement socks.

I left the house to the howls of the dogs, which had been locked up for my benefit, and drove the Valiant back to my office in Darlinghurst, where I rang Lizzie Darcy at her newspaper.

'I see the Labor Party's given your boyfriend the arse,' I said, unkindly.

Lizzie's boyfriend was a backroom boy who'd got caught up in the bloodbath that followed Labor's defeat after twelve years of running New South Wales like the Bayside Branch.

'He resigned,' she said.

I blew a raspberry. 'So did Richard Nixon.'

Mistake. 'What do you want, Fishface?' she asked, colder than a socialite's heart. 'I'm busy.'

I told her.

'Denise Dwyer? You must remember her. She was our very own porn queen. Coogan discovered she had... certain skills. He turned her into a minor cult figure and made a fortune out of her, then she suddenly dropped out of sight. Can't help you with the family, though. There must be millions of Dwyers.'

'Somebody must know Denise's family,' I persisted.

She thought for a while and I could hear her puffing on a cigarette though she'd sworn she'd given them up ages ago. 'Dwyers are usually Catholics, aren't they?'

'Most likely. Or they started out that way.'

'Give me an hour or so, will you? I'll make some inquiries. Where will you be?'

Figuring I might as well have an early lunch, I went to a nearby cafe. The sardine salad didn't tempt me, so I had sausages and chips and a chat with Tina, the Greek waitress, who bashed my ears about her son who lay about watching television all day.

'It could be worse,' I said. 'I'm working for a bloke whose boy's been kidnapped.'

'How come that man gets all the luck?' she lamented slamming down a bowl of tinned fruit salad and ice cream.

Back at the office, Lizzie called and told me she'd set up a meeting with an old friend of hers, a semi-retired priest who had a line on every Irish Catholic in Sydney. He also had an extensive network of political hacks, writers, trade unionists, journalists and bureaucrats. A reliable source, indeed.

I met Declan Doherty in a coffee shop in Park Street. Subsequently I discovered he knew every coffee shop in the greater metropolitan area, plus all the bookshops, movie houses and theatres. He was in mufti, with a dark jacket and crewneck jumper and black sneakers for city walking. We ordered coffee and toast. I didn't know it then but it was the beginning of a long and fruitful association.

He checked me out carefully and said: 'Marist Brothers Darlinghurst, wasn't it?'

I nodded.

'I knew your uncle Reg during the War. In New Guinea.'

He was showing off, but it was a class act, nonetheless. I asked him about Denise.

'Denise Dwyer. Yes. A tragic tale, that. As I recall, the family broke up when she was a child. The mother died when Denise was in primary school and the father disappeared. She went to live with her grandmother. A beautiful girl, but she went right off the rails. It wasn't the grandmother's fault; she just wasn't up to it.'

'Lizzie tells me she got mixed up with Bernie Coogan and he put her in his home movies.'

His face wrinkled with disgust. 'Ah, yes, Bernie Coogan. A terrible man.' He glanced at me shrewdly: 'Is he looking for Denise?'

'He wants me to talk to her.'

'Do you think that would be a good idea?'

'They had a son,' I told him. 'Denise went underground years ago, when the boy was a baby. Coogan wants to find the boy but he has to find Denise first. I thought her relatives might know where she was.'

He seemed doubtful. 'The boy might be better off without Bernie Coogan.'

'Yeah, but Coogan's the kid's father, so I suppose he's got some rights.'

'He didn't feel the need to exercise them before this,' said the old priest. 'Why now?'

'His wife is expecting a baby,' I said. 'Perhaps it's aroused his paternal instincts.'

He snorted, but he was still listening. I pressed my advantage. 'If Coogan wants to make it up to his son, surely we shouldn't stand in his way, Father? And besides, he's a very rich man...'

He didn't believe a word of it but he couldn't resist a mystery. There was a good yarn in this, and he figured he'd squeeze it out of me eventually. Then he could dine out on it for a year.

He capitulated. 'Denise lived with her grandmother in Rozelle, her maternal grandmother, Nellie Davies. I don't know if she'd still be alive, though. She'd be a great age by now.'

I remained hopeful, these little old Irish battlers live forever.

We chatted for a while, mostly about movies, which he was addicted to, and he picked my brains about my trade. As I was paying, I said: 'By the way, this is highly confidential.'

He was offended: 'Of course, of course. I wouldn't dream of telling anyone.' Apart from his hundred closest friends.

We took a taxi to Darlinghurst to pick up the Valiant, and I dropped him off at the Apia Club to lunch with his brother and plug into another week's worth of scuttlebut.

Nellie Davies lived in one of Rozelle's many narrow, treeless streets bordered by little wooden houses. This was authentic working-class Sydney, with too many dogs, the races on every trannie on Saturday afternoons, noisy kids, and few expectations beyond a late model Japanese car and winning the trifecta just once.

Number thirteen was freshly painted and well kept, with a neat garden and a tabby cat asleep on the front steps. Nellie Davies was over eighty, small and white haired, but alert and spry. She was dying for a gossip. While she made me a cup of tea, I told her I worked for a bank that was trying to locate customers who hadn't operated their accounts for two years. We wanted to give their money back, I said, carefully keeping my face straight.

Nellie Davies believed me: she probably didn't read the financial pages of the newspaper. She told me Denise was a bit disorganised about money but very generous; she sent her grandmother money regularly, and had paid to get the house painted.

I noticed some photos on the mantlepiece and picked up a family group: 'Nice looking family. Is this Denise?'

'Yes. And that's her husband Des and Denise's son, Luke.'

Denise was beautiful, with long, straight, sandy hair and grey eyes. She'd put on a bit of weight since her movie star days but carried it well. The kid, with his mother's blond hair and faded denim eyes, had the sultry good looks of a teenage rock star. And not a pustule in sight.

The old lady told me Luke had spent his last two Christmas holidays in Coogee with the family of a boy he'd met through his football club. He often popped over to see her, she said. A very nice boy.

I left full of strong tea and cream sponge, with Denise's address in Newcastle and a vague sense of regret that I no longer had a grannie tucked away somewhere baking Anzac biscuits and telling visitors how wonderful I was. I had also souvenired a snapshot of Luke in his football gear. The kid was athletic as well as handsome. Look out girls.

I rang Coogan's house and got the breathless Michele and asked her to tell Bernie I'd located Denise and was going to Newcastle to check it out. Talking to the girl was like pulling teeth. I couldn't make up my mind whether she was terrified of Bernie or just plain stupid. Or both.

I survived the pall of yellow chemicals hanging over Newcastle and took the skybridge to Stockton Beach. It's more fun by ferry but I didn't have the time. Parking the Valiant, I walked along the beach in the sun, stopping to watch a ship looming up ahead, close enough to touch, on its way into Newcastle Harbour.

Stockton Beach was old-fashioned and a bit seedy, with peeling weatherboard houses and holiday flats, a big caravan park and the steelworks within sight; it had a slow easy feeling, as if time had stopped there in the fifties. The beach was excellent, and where else could you sit on your own balcony sucking on a tinnie and watching your ship come in?

I found Denise's house and knocked. She came to the door in jeans and a tee shirt, tanned, no makeup: she didn't need it. A blast of pure femaleness made me step back involuntarily.

Denise's photograph didn't do her justice. She had the kind of effortless, languid sex appeal that turns grown men into boys and makes boys howl.

I told Denise I was from Luke's school, that we wanted to contact his family about putting up an athlete from an American high school team in the new year. She asked me in.

It was a pretty ordinary house, but she'd made it homey with a big old velvet couch, lots of plants, and more interestingly, framed religious texts. Somebody in the house had got religion in a big way.

Denise made me a cup of tea and we chatted about the visiting team, and I asked her where Luke was. In Sydney, staying with a friend, she said; the mother sounded very nice on the phone. I wondered how Denise would react when she found out the golden boy had defected to the pornographer, but I certainly wasn't going to be the one to tell her.

If Denise was in on this scam, she was an excellent actress, and blue movies didn't exactly demand highly developed dramatic skills. Eyeing off the exhortations to be good, I decided I was wasting time with Denise. There was always Des Cochrane, though.

Obligingly, Des walked in. Denise lit up at the sight of him, and he was certainly an excellent specimen. Big, dark and muscular, he was obviously a shift worker at the steel mill. He wasn't pleased to see me. I couldn't blame him: if I had Denise at home, I'd have the house patrolled night and day by security guards, preferably female.

While she flapped around making him a fresh pot of tea, taking every opportunity to brush against him, Denise filled Des in on the reason for my visit. Something set off alarm bells in Des. When he started cross-examining me, I made excuses and got out of there fast. As I was walking towards my car, I looked back and saw him watching me from the verandah.

When he went inside, I changed course and dropped in at a pub at the end of the street to see if I could find out more about Des, and besides, it was almost cocktail hour.

My sense of *déjà vu* intensified in the pub, where the fifties feeling was so strong I succumbed to nostalgia and played some early Elvis on the jukebox. I was immediately accosted by a well-upholstered middle-aged woman with an enormous bosom, a bad perm and more makeup than Marcel Marceau.

'Wasn't he lovely?' she moaned, bathing me in sherry fumes.

'Who?'

'Elvis, silly.'

'Yeah,' I said. 'Lovely.' Before he turned into the Great White Whale, that is.

'He was such a nice boy, too. Such a gentleman.'

'Yeah, he certainly loved his mother.'

'It was all the Colonel's fault,' she told me.

'Absolutely,' I agreed.

'I just loved him in *Blue Hawaii*,' she said.

'*King Creole* was better,' I opined.

We were having a fine argument when Des Cochrane came in. He looked around, saw me, pulled up a chair, signalled for a beer, and said: 'Piss off, Noela,' in one fluid motion.

'You're such a bully, Des,' simpered Noela, but she went. Soon after I heard *Love Me Tender* oozing from the box.

'What's going on?' asked Des, when he'd got his beer and the curious barman was out of earshot.

'What do you mean?'

'Look, I didn't believe any of that crap you were giving Denise. What's it all about?'

I stalled.

'I'm not going to tell Denise, if that's what you're worried about,' he said. 'I love Denise. She's had enough shit in her life already. If something bad is going to happen, I want to know about it.'

By this time I'd made up my mind nobody in Stockton Beach had anything to do with Luke's disappearance, so I told him. He was flabbergasted. 'Staying with Coogan after what that bastard did to his mother? Jesus! The kid's wild, but I didn't think he was that...'

'Devious?' I prompted.

He put down his glass, and a youth came and picked it up. I'd noticed him hovering in the background, but I suddenly realised he'd been listening in. I gave him the hard eye and he scuttled away.

'How bad is this?' asked Des, remembering Luke was missing. 'Is the kid really in danger, or is this one of Coogan's numbers?'

I said it looked serious.

'Shouldn't someone be calling the cops?' he demanded.

I told Des Coogan wanted to handle it himself, and that he probably had a better chance of springing the kid than the cops did; he had equal firepower and fewer scruples. I didn't add that calling the cops would do me out of twenty grand.

Cochrane left after making me promise to call him at work as soon as I had any good news. Denise had apparently learned a lesson with Coogan and had done better the second time: Des was a rough diamond, but he doted on her and had apparently done his best with her son.

As soon as Des was out of sight, the kid reappeared. He was fresh-faced and ungainly, still growing into his body. His hair looked as if someone had cut it with a knife and fork, and he had pimples and that furry-faced look some kids get when the hormones start popping.

'Can I talk to you?' he asked.

'Talk,' I said.

He looked around nervously, but the bar was almost empty and those who were left seemed comatose. Even Noela had gone. Nobody was interested in us.

'I'm a friend of Luke's,' he said. 'Has something happened to him?'

'Nothing you can do anything about.'

He flushed: I'd hurt his pride. 'I know a few things you don't,' he growled.

'Like what?'

'I know where he's been staying in Sydney.'

He'd finally aroused my interest. 'What was he up to, do you know? Was he looking for his long-lost father, or was he after a share of Bernie's loot?'

The kid was loyal; he bit. 'He hated Coogan for what he'd done to his mum!'

'Denise told him?'

'Yeah, Denise got born again a few years ago and confessed. And I think she wanted him to know in case somebody else told him. So he'd be ready.'

I could see Denise's point. It wouldn't be easy having a pornographer for a father and a Linda Lovelace clone for a mother.

I said to the kid: 'If you know what he was up to in Coogee, you'd better tell me, son. It might be important.'

'I think he wanted to get revenge.'

'How?'

The kid admitted he didn't know. I thought Luke's character might give me some ideas, so I quizzed him about his friend.

'He's a bit mixed up, I suppose. He goes off half-cocked sometimes and stuffs things up. But he's not bad, he's not...'

'Evil?'

'No, not like Coogan. He's more like his mum. Denise is a good lady.'

I smiled. It must have been sheer torture for pubescent boys to be around Denise. It was bad enough for me.

I thanked him and and got up to leave. He sat on.

'What?' I asked.

He swallowed hard. 'I think there was something else going on, something about a girl.'

Before I could grill him further, somebody yelled 'Scott!' and the boy jumped up guiltily and went back to collecting glasses. A good kid, a good friend. It was unlikely that a girlfriend had kidnapped Luke, but I filed away the scrap of information just in case.

Kidnappers were thin on the ground in the Hunter, so I went back to Sydney and called in on Coogan. Michele let me in with less ado this time, but she wasn't looking any better and had black circles under her eyes.

I told Coogan I didn't think Luke's family were mixed up in the kidnapping, but I didn't say anything about telling Des, or the revenge angle. Coogan said he hadn't been able to find a single lead in Sydney. He'd leaned on all the likely informants, but nobody was talking. Doubtless a few spare toes would turn up in Sydney rubbish tins in the next few days.

'I'm stuffed if I know what's going on,' he complained.

I was in the same boat. 'There's something weird about the whole thing,' I said. 'Something doesn't add up.'

Coogan went away to answer the phone, and I tried to pump Michele, who was pouring coffee. 'Was Luke involved with a girl, Michele?'

Michele spilled coffee in her lap, gasped, and jumped up. I tried to wipe her dress with a napkin, but she slapped my hand away.

At that point Coogan came in and said: 'What's going on? What happened, Michele?'

By this time Michele was weeping and dabbing at her dress with a Kleenex. She didn't answer.

'I was just asking her about Luke,' I explained. 'I wondered if he'd got in too deep with some girl.'

'Well? Stop bawling and talk, Michele!' barked Coogan. 'Was there some trouble with a girlfriend?'

'I don't know,' she wailed. 'If there was, he didn't tell me about it. Leave me alone, for God's sake!' She ran out of the room.

'Save me from bloody pregnant women,' said Coogan.

'Is she fond of Luke?' I asked.

'I don't know. But I'm away a lot, so I suppose he was company for her.'

Leaving Coogan to man the phones, I left the house and got into the Valiant to go back to town. Exhausted by the long trip to the Hunter, it refused to start. I called Coogan and we peered under the bonnet and fiddled with a few wires. Nothing happened, of course, we were both mechanical morons.

Finally Coogan said: 'Leave it here and I'll get it...'

'Not one of your tow truck mates, for Christ's sake,' I pleaded. 'I love this car.'

He roared laughing. 'Don't get your tits in a knot, sweetheart. I'll get a mechanic in to have a look at it.'

After reading me the riot act about getting it back in mint condition, Coogan lent me his Porsche. It hurt, though: he was the kind of tight-fisted bastard who kept the sixpences out of Christmas puddings and invested them.

I like to think I'm above vulgar consumerism, but I could feel the car turning me into an arrogant parvenu as soon as I slipped behind the steering wheel. All I needed now was driving gloves, streaked hair and Raybans.

As I slid through the electronic security gates a sinister black Saab Turbo with tinted windows pulled out behind me. Sitting well back, it cruised as relentlessly as a shark. But was it after me or Coogan? I didn't care: I had no intention of becoming the consolation prize.

So I certainly wasn't going to lead them into my territory. I considered leading them straight to 14 College Street, but there were certain difficulties involved. The police were likely to be curious about a PI driving a vice king's car, for starters. The flash of a newspaper poster on the roadside screaming Fitzgerald Corruptions Revelations gave me the answer.

With my pursuers sticking closer than dogshit to a Reebok, I flew down Oxford Street, left into Wentworth Avenue, right into Eddy Avenue, left into Pitt, through Broadway, adding to the congestion and stink, threw a right into Wattle, right into Thomas, and another right into Jones Street. They were falling for it.

Hoping nobody would steal the car, I double-parked like everyone else, ran across the road, hoons in pursuit, through the vestibule, vaguely heard the commissionaire shouting, pushed open the fire door and took off up the stairs. Fear gave me wings.

Spurred on by the noise of pounding feet behind me, I exploded into the fourth floor lobby, charged past the protesting receptionist and flung myself into Lizzie's office. A sudden hush fell over the computer terminals as three red-faced, gasping strangers burst in. Conversations were suspended, computers lay idle and phones went unanswered.

Suddenly realising where they were, the bloodhounds screeched to a halt. 'Bloody hell,' one muttered.

Safe behind the desk of a shell-shocked female lifestyle reporter, I finally had the opportunity to identify the goons. The leader was Rory Callaghan, a notorious Irish kneecapper, branch stacker and procurer for politicians. His steroid-stoked sidekick was unfamiliar.

It wasn't until he'd entered the brightly-lit room that Callaghan realised he wasn't chasing Bernie Coogan. He quickly recovered his aplomb, gave me a hard look from his pale, froggy eyes, smoothed down his crewcut, jerked his head towards the door and led the way out.

At their exit an excited babble broke out but the journos gave me a wide berth. Nobody asked me my name or suggested I leave. Callaghan and his associates have that sort of effect on law-abiding citizens with kids and mortgages.

As I was deciding it was safe to venture into the streets again, Lizzie strode past, hissing through clenched teeth: 'Get out of here, you... hoon!'

I left. Any half-formed idea I'd had about keeping the incident quiet evaporated when I saw the Porsche's headlights. I re-entered the lobby, ate crow, and used the doorman's phone to call Bernie. He called a towtruck and arrived in a pink Porsche with MICHELE plates, abused me, wept over the car and hassled the shit out of the brunos on the truck. They took it: Bernie had a reputation in the industry.

When he calmed down enough to talk sense, I asked him if

Callaghan could be behind the snatch. He was astonished at my naivety: 'Rory is a professional, Fish. We have our disagreements, but he's not stupid enough to hurt my family. This little argument is none of your business.'

Suitably chastened, I grabbed a cab on Broadway and went home. Too overwrought to sleep, I watched some TV and stewed about the case. Bernie's conviction that Callaghan was too smart to threaten his family rang true. Most professional crims steer clear of kidnappings because they're notoriously difficult to carry off — the cops hate kidnappers and pull out all stops, and juries tend to lock them up and throw away the key.

The logic in this case was definitely screwy, and I was starting to get some very strange ideas, dangerous ideas.

Maybe somebody could tie up some loose ends for me. I racked my brains and came up with the name of the pub in Stockton Beach and put in a call. They finally found Scott, who answered suspiciously.

'Listen, Scott, and listen good,' I said. 'Bernie Coogan is big league. People who stuff around with him end up walking with sticks. Or dead.' I paused for effect: 'Was Luke in some sort of mess with this girl you told me about?'

'Well, he said if his father found out, he'd kill him.'

'Did he mean it, or was he just big-noting?'

'I think he meant it. He was really scared.'

Now, Bernie Coogan didn't give a damn about the welfare of the rest of the human race, and he'd find the whole subject of wild oats irresistibly funny; I decided to have a heart-to-heart with Michele.

I called the mansion and told her we had to talk. She was unwilling but invited me up.

'No,' I said. 'This is kind of delicate. I think you should meet me at the Sebel Townhouse. In the piano bar. Soon.'

I'd considered the Coogee pubs, but they catered exclusively to bar brawlers, Maori bouncers and drug dealers: no place for pregnant women.

'What's this about?' Michele demanded.

'I think you and I need to talk about your stepson. I think he's been pulling girls' pants down, and I thought we might be able to figure out a course of action.'

There was a silence, then she said: 'All right, I'll come.'

As she climbed out of the pink Porsche in front of the hotel, I caught a flash of long brown leg and white panties, and realised, somewhat belatedly, that Michele was a very pretty girl, in a suburban Dallas kind of way. No match for Denise but a later model. She still looked tired, but had painted some colour into her face, touched up the red in her hair and was wearing a low-cut sundress that showed off her tan.

She ordered a gin and tonic.

'Should you be drinking?' I asked. 'It's going to be rough enough for this kid without being born with a drinking problem.'

She went dead white and I thought she might faint. 'You're a real bastard, aren't you?' she whispered.

'Maybe,' I conceded. 'But I'm basically non-violent and I don't want to see anybody get shot, even accidentally. So I think you'd better tell me all about it.'

Playing for time, Michele took a long draught of g and t, all the time watching me, figuring the odds. She needed a nudge: I gave it: 'I could always call Bernie and invite him over...'

It worked: 'He shouldn't have left us alone so much!' So it was all Bernie's fault.

'I'm not interested in the Mills and Boon part,' I interrupted. 'I just want to know how you thought you were going to get away with this.'

'I've been taking the calls,' she said. 'I was going to deliver the money. We didn't expect Bernie to call you in. I thought he'd be too mingy to pay for help.'

'You don't like him,' I said.

'He's a pig.'

'You married him.'

'Yeah, well it seemed like a good idea at the time. I was getting desperate. Bernie seemed like a way out. And I've done some pretty awful men in my time; I thought I could handle it.'

'What went wrong?'

She gulped down some gin, hiccoughed unhappily and said: 'I

dunno, maybe it was the red fur. He's even got red hair on his back.'

Fortunately I stopped myself from laughing, because Michele hadn't finished: 'And I got lonely. Bernie never takes me anywhere. He likes making money and playing pool with his fat friends and watching dirty movies on the bloody video. I'm twenty-three years old. I'm too young to die.'

'You could have left.'

She laughed bleakly. 'Back to doing perms all day in some suburban hairdresser's and getting dermatitis and varicose veins, you mean? I'd rather put up with Bernie.'

'But this baby,' I said. 'I don't get it.'

'It was an accident. I'd been trying for two years with Bernie and nothing happened, so I figured I couldn't have kids. Then Luke came along, and whammo!'

'You didn't consider, uh, getting rid of it?'

'Why should I? Bernie would never know the difference, and anyway, it's my little insurance policy.'

'What about this kidnapping plot?' I urged.

'That was Luke's idea. When he found out about the baby he got all territorial. He wanted me to run away with him.'

'On Bernie's money?'

'Yes.'

'Half a million bucks is a lot of travel money.'

'Bernie's got it,' she said. 'But that was only part of it. I think Luke wanted to give some of it to Denise because of the way Bernie had treated her. He was very bitter about that. He despises Bernie.'

'Luke's only sixteen years old, for Christ's sake,' I said. 'Didn't you try to talk him out of it?'

'Of course! I told him he was mad. I said Bernie would break both his legs, or worse. And God knows what he'd do to me...'

'You'll have to call it off now,' I said. 'Bernie will kill Luke if he catches him picking up the dough.'

'I know. I've been so scared it's been making me bilious. But he's such a wild kid. I couldn't stop him. He said if I didn't go along with him, he'd tell Bernie about us, about the baby.'

Like father, like son, I thought.

She looked at me with big, hopeless brown eyes: 'What are you going to do?'

I could see my twenty grand receding rapidly, like a mirage, but I didn't want to be an accessory to murder or aggravated assault, so I started thinking laterally: 'Get in touch with Luke. Tell him to get himself bashed up — that shouldn't be too hard around Coogee — and to get some rope burns on his wrists. Then he should come home and tell Bernie's he's escaped. The story is he's been kept on a boat and he got away and swam ashore.'

I was winging it, trying to anticipate what Bernie would swallow: 'And he can't describe any of the kidnappers because he was blindfolded. Maybe he'd been drugged. Yeah, he was drugged. Can you remember all this?'

She nodded.

'And tell him to stick to his story. If he starts getting fancy, he'll contradict himself. Bernie's no fool. And you pull yourself together and be very, very cool when Luke turns up. Do you understand?'

She understood. Michele wasn't superbright, but she knew which side her bread was buttered on. I gave her thirty cents and pointed her at a phone.

After she'd left, I called Coogan and asked him what was happening. Nothing, he told me. He hadn't heard from the kidnappers yet. He asked me over. I sat drinking for a while, waiting for Michele to get home, wondering if the young lovers would have the nerve to pull this off. I hoped Luke had inherited his father's rat cunning.

Up at the house Coogan barbecued steaks and we drank red wine and listened to some old Motown music (even pornographers aren't all bad) and waited. Michele had perked up now the suspense was almost over and ate a steak.

'Eating for two,' said Coogan, pointing at her belly with a forkful of meat, and Michele blushed.

The kid staggered in eventually, bedraggled and bruised. His eyes flicked quickly over me and rested for a moment on Michele, who was clutching my arm and twanging with fear.

Luke was a big bugger, with a footballer's neck and legs, but with just enough baby fat on his face to make him irresistible to women. Even tired, dirty and scared, he was bursting with vitality. I could understand Michele landing in his lap; I just couldn't understand Coogan being stupid enough to throw them together.

As Luke stumbled through his story, Coogan came as close as I'd ever seen to expressing an emotion. He hugged the boy and plied him with whisky and they went upstairs arm in arm to run a bath.

'What now?' I asked Michele, who was weak with relief.

'God knows. What would you do?'

'I'd piss Luke off home to Des for a good thrashing, plead nervous exhaustion and take a long holiday.'

'I love him,' she said.

'Stop while you're ahead, Michele,' I warned. 'Don't do anything stupid.'

'Anything more, you mean.' She came over and gave me a hug. 'You're not so tough, Syd.'

Michele wasn't a bad girl, just lazy, and I had a feeling she was a survivor. Coogan's women had a way of turning out stronger than he'd expected.

'Just keep your chin up, your mouth shut and your tits stuck out, and you'll be OK,' I advised, and we laughed and I went home.

I remembered to call Des at the steelworks to tell him Luke was home safe, that it was all over. I said the boy had some explaining to do, to Denise and his grandmother.

'Not to mention me,' said Des grimly. Luke wasn't out of the woods yet.

Coogan paid me for two days' work plus a generous consolation prize. He was getting soft: in the old days he would have deducted the cost of the steak. He even thanked me, the poor deluded bastard, but they say love is blind.

A couple of weeks later I got a call from Des to tell me Luke and Denise had patched it up after some initial hysteria and recriminations. Christian forgiveness had won out. Luke was going to be allowed to stay with Bernie whenever he wanted to, though I wondered if his enthusiasm for Coogee hadn't waned a little since his close shave.

Soon after I was ambushed by Declan Doherty in Castlereagh Street and we found a coffee shop. 'I trust the Coogan matter worked out satisfactorily?' he asked.

'Very. Coogan and Denise are talking again after sixteen years and sharing custody of the kid. Couldn't have hoped for a better outcome.'

'I hear Luke is a very nice looking lad,' he said casually. 'Not like Bernie at all.'

My scalp began to prickle: 'He's like Denise.'

'Oh,' he said, ordering more toast. He munched busily. 'There was some talk at the time, you know. She was seen around with Alan Drury quite a lot.'

In 1974 Alan Drury was tall, blond and one of the most talented front row forwards around. I started to laugh, inhaled a crumb and had to be slapped on the back.

The priest was solicitous. 'Are you all right, Sydney? I hope I haven't upset you.'

'Not at all,' I said. 'Not at all,' and looked up to see him smiling like Savonarola.

Two Dog Night

The Wahroonga house was a phony English-looking job with gables and the inevitable BMW in the driveway. Inside, the good taste was professionally prepackaged, but the house felt unloved, unlived in. When I met the owner I realised why: nobody home there either.

Whichever way you looked at it, Hamish McLeod was a pompous ass. I was looking at it in his study over the rim of a heavy crystal glass of Chivas. The room featured leather chairs with buttons, a state of the art personal computer and lots of unread looking hardbacks about statesmen, explorers and captains of industry. He probably holed up in here to read *Penthouse* and pick his nose.

The man himself was wearing a tailormade suit designed to look old-fashioned and cover the ravages of too many expense account lunches. Combined with rimless glasses, it made him look like one of Ben Chifley's aides.

My critical appraisal was interrupted by McLeod's fat fruity voice. 'It's a custody case...' he began.

I groaned. The space between divorcing couples is like the Somme, littered with the bodies of the innocent and the foolhardy. It would take more than a shot of whisky to make me go over the top.

'...of a sort,' he finished patiently, making a pyramid of his podgy manicured fingers. He blasted a pipeful of Dunhill at me and I coughed weakly.

'What sort?' I demanded.

'The objects of the dispute are canine,' he said.

'Dogs?! You're having a custody battle over dogs?'

'Two dogs, to be precise.'

'Big dogs? Savage dogs? German dogs?' As an inner-city dweller, I'm not all that fond of dogs.

'Oh, no. Well, biggish, but not savage. Definitely not savage. On the contrary, they're very friendly.'

He opened his antique desk and took out a leather framed snapshot of a woman and two English sheepdogs.

'Stan and Ollie,' he said, and I nearly choked on my Chivas.

At least one member of the family had a sense of humour. I examined her photograph.

Fiona McLeod had long brown hair, Carly Simon teeth, legs like Linda Rondstadt's before she got fat, and a definite glint in her eye. I wondered how she'd stuck it out so long with the Young Winston.

'I take it your wife wants the dogs?'

'My wife has the dogs, Mr Fish. I want them back.'

'Whose dogs are they?'

'I paid for them,' he said. 'They're mine.'

His faith in logic was touching. He'd probably bought Fiona too, and she wasn't his any more.

'I get the feeling Mrs McLeod isn't going to just hand the dogs to me on a platter,' I said. 'How do you want me to go about getting them back?'

'I want you to use your judgment.'

The man wasn't going to be nailed for conspiracy in any dognapping (imagine how it would look in *Australian Business*). He was probably taping the whole interview.

'It'll cost you,' I warned, mentally factoring in rabies, fleas, the indignity of it all and the glint in Fiona McLeod's eye.

He named a fee. I sat tight. He cracked and raised it. Now I had some idea how much he wanted to punish his wife, I demanded a bonus of five thousand dollars on delivery of the dogs safe and well. He paled, protested and capitulated. I was bought.

'So where are Stan and Ollie and Mrs McLeod?'

'I don't know. She's gone underground.'

'Who does she know who doesn't like you and has room for two big dogs?' I asked.

He got out his Mont Blanc and wrote me a list: Lucy Le Gay, friend, Palm Beach; Ambrose Pierce, brother, Double Bay; Mary Woods, mother, Glen Innes. The brother lived in an apartment, so it had to be Palm Beach or Glen Innes, and knowing my luck... I pointed to the mother's name and raised my eyebrows.

'Fiona's mother remarried,' he said. 'A farmer. They have a property outside Glen Innes.'

'Is she likely to go to her mother's?' I asked.

'It's a very close family,' he said sourly, and I wondered.

'I need a cover,' I said. 'What does Fiona do?'

'Fiona shops.'

'Before she got married,' I prompted.

'She was an airline stewardess with Qantas.'

Evidently Singapore girls weren't the only great way to fly. 'When was this?'

'Eighty to eighty-six.'

He saw me out through the cheerless house and said: 'Mr Fish, Fiona is no fool.' He coughed: 'And she has an extensive knowledge of male psychology.'

Fiona McLeod was beginning to interest me. I needed a bit of excitement in my life. First Palm Beach, hangout of silvertails and surfers, and more recently, reclusive heroin dealers and bestseller writers.

Lucy Le Gay's house was what the locals like to call a shack. In this part of the world a shack starts at about half a million.

There was no answer at the front door but I found the owner in the garden. I introduced myself and told her I was looking for Fiona McLeod for a feature on ex-stewardesses for the Qantas magazine.

'Did you ask her husband?'

'Mr McLeod seems to have lost touch with his wife,' I said. 'He gave me your name.'

'Poor Hamish,' she said. She took off her gardening gloves and brushed her hair back. 'It's hot. I could use a drink. Care to join me? Or are you one of those dreary people who won't touch alcohol before sunset?'

'What sun?' I said.

She led me to the sort of verandah they used to build, with old cane furniture, potted palms and views of the sea.

Trying not to do too much full frontal staring, I watched her as she made drinks and rustled up some nuts. Lucy Le Gay had browny-gold wavy hair cut to show off her long neck, green eyes, a pale tan and good cheekbones. She was small-boned and light on her feet like a dancer.

Fiona was with her mother in Glen Innes, she told me. She asked casually about Hamish, but obviously wanted to know all the dirt. 'Did he say anything about Fiona?'

'No,' I lied. 'I got the impression there was no love lost between them, but he didn't give away much. 'He's a pretty cold fish.'

'Cold men are the most dangerous sort,' she said, and I sensed a story.

'You worked with Fiona?' I asked, well into my second gin and tonic.

'Yes, at Qantas.'

'Tell me why an intelligent woman would want to be a flying tealady,' I said.

'It was a damned sight better than being a doctor's receptionist and marrying a bank clerk and moving into the same street as your parents,' she said. 'And let's face it, where else would you meet that many men?'

'And you met Mr Right on QF11?'

'In Singapore, to be exact.'

'It seems to have worked out fine,' I said, surveying the spoils.

She didn't answer for a while, then seemed to come to a decision: she needed someone to talk to. Someone male. It must have been one of my teddybear days.

'Yes and no,' she said. 'I've got the house, but I don't know if I've still got the man. Or if I even want him. My husband disappeared three years ago on a business trip. In the Philippines, as far as the police can tell. He might be dead.'

'I take it he wasn't selling office equipment?'

'I never asked. I suppose I was afraid. If I'd known, I would have had to do something.'

'Like go to the cops?'

'Oh, no. I could never do that. It's so complicated...'

Lots of unfinished business there.

When she wrenched herself back from the past, she said: 'I did a lot of thinking when Jean Paul went missing. Once I put all the pieces together I realised he must have been trafficking. And I'd been living on the profits. I had some sort of crackup.'

She seemed calm as the Buddha to me, with the sea and the garden. 'You seem to have worked it out.'

'Almost... But I didn't do it by myself. Fiona dragged me through it. She's very strong.'

'You're close friends?'

'That's the strange part. We weren't all that close at Qantas. But Fiona rang me up one night out of the blue when I was desperate for someone to talk to. She probably saved my life.'

This didn't sound like the woman in the photo: 'What was in it for Fiona?'

'I think she needed someone to care about. She felt useless, I think.'

'You mean Hamish wasn't enough.'

She said: 'It was strange, that: Fiona and Hamish, I mean. It was all wrong... But then, so was my marriage.'

She got up and walked to the railing and leaned over. I admired her legs.

'You know what pulled me through, Syd? I sat at home for months listening to music, thinking about my life and making a patchwork quilt. It was a sort of meditation, I suppose. I sewed all the hurt and anger and guilt into that quilt. You should try it some time.'

'I can't sew,' I said. It lightened us both up and we started to laugh.

I was living dangerously again, falling in love with Lucy Le Gay and planning to steal her best friend's best friends. But then, I needed the money, and unless Fiona spotted me, Lucy would never find out...

The twilight advanced but we lingered on, unwilling to move and break the spell. It was straight out of Somerset Maugham — cocktails and sexual tension on a verandah at dusk.

When it got too dark, she went inside, lit a couple of lamps, turned on FM classical and returned with some dope.

'Do you do this?'

'When the mood is right,' I said.

I watched as she rolled some joints with small brown hands: she wasn't wearing a wedding ring. We had a smoke and talked softly, filling in bits of our pasts. She used her hands when she talked, and I must have been staring at them, because she flushed suddenly and folded them in her lap. I'd have to learn to watch my eyes.

'You smoke much of this stuff?' I asked.

'Sometimes. Daydreams are better than nightmares.'

'When Jean Paul went?'

'Yes. And when I started to realise who he was. And who I was.'

Such melancholy in her voice. She'd kicked off her sandals and put one bare foot on the coffee table. I leaned over and picked it up and stroked it, and ran my tongue along the soft inside of her sole, watching her face.

'Oh!' she whispered, and her eyes closed.

She said: 'Syd, I haven't done this for such a long time...'

I began to understand then how hard Lucy had to work to maintain how fragile she was. 'I've got all the time in the world,' I said, and moved onto the couch beside her.

She leaned into me and I played with her pretty fingers.

'I'd really like to see that patchwork quilt,' I said, and she laughed and it meant yes.

'You've got a lovely strong back, Syd,' she said, watching me undress silhouetted against the window.

Lucy was small but perfectly proportioned, and the curve from breast to hip was a roller coaster ride. The skin on her body was fine and smooth: I tasted every inch of it. And she had the most wonderful smell, very light with a musky undernote — the sort of perfume you can't buy in bottles. She came to me with enormous relief, as if I'd rescued her from a desert island. With Lucy I felt strong and protective: nobody could make me feel honest.

Later she said: 'I need lots of hugging, Syd,' and we lay intertwined for hours under her patchwork quilt. It was a work of art; subtle, intricate, and finely made, with Lucy in every stitch.

When I left next morning, I felt much better disposed towards Hamish McLeod.

It's a long way to Glen Innes, on the inland route, up Highway 15, through the Hunter, country and western land and Armidale, where I had the best steak in Australia at the Bowling Club.

The countryside around Glen Innes was green and lush, a tribute to Scottish hard work and Australian agronomy. I like to think I could drop out to one of these country towns: everything seems simpler there, but it's probably an illusion—people shoot each other a lot in the bush.

The town itself was perfectly preserved, a movie set for a Chips Rafferty film. The streets were wide, their pre-war façades intact; the people were Anglo-Saxon, Protestant and prosperous. On a Saturday morning the shopping centre was jumping with country folk spending money and tapping into the bush telegraph.

The cakeshops had real pies and sausage rolls, and I even found a passable espresso. As I was soaking up the caffeine and the local colour, Fiona McLeod, her mother and the two Disney dogs walked by. They were a little too glamorous for Glen Innes, as if they'd strayed out of a Country Road catalogue.

In person Fiona McLeod was striking in a North Shore brunette way, athletic and confident. She laughed a lot. Her marriage might be broken, but her heart appeared to be intact. Mother and daughter seemed to be good friends.

Eventually they drove off in a white station wagon, with me in tow. They led me to a thriving farm with a big white farmhouse with green shutters and roof and lots of old trees. The stepfather came out to meet them and carry parcels—he looked more authentic, denim shirt and a battered hat—and they disappeared inside.

I was too conspicuous here, so I drove back to the highway and parked under some trees. It was boring and I was hungry, and absolutely nothing happened. I revised my fantasy about going bush. The radio waves were full of hillbilly music and schlock rock, so I played some Benny Goodman to keep myself awake, and did the crossword in an ancient newspaper I found on the floor of the back seat.

Saturday night saw me marooned in a pub, faced with the choice of the town bore who told me how the proposed new gun laws would restrict his civil liberties, an ageing country and western singer with a sob in her voice, and soaps on regional TV. I gave up and went back to my motel room and rang Lizzie Darcy on the off-chance.

'What are you doing alone on a Saturday night?' I asked.

'Thanks, Syd. That really makes me feel better. Getting drunk of course, how about you?'

'I'm still sober. The pubs are too depressing. All that talk about dieback and blight. I expected Hanrahan to walk in any minute and tell us we'd all be ruined.'

'Where are you!?'

'Glen Innes.'

'Glen Innes! What are you going there?'

I told her. 'Dognapping! Jesus, Syd, I thought you'd hit rock-bottom working for a Liberal politician.'

I chose not to respond to that. 'I can't get near the bloody dogs anyway. They're holed up on the Woods' farm. And old Woods looks like the kind of bloke who'd shoot anyone he caught trying to lift his livestock.'

'Shooting is too good for dog duffers,' said Lizzie, enjoying herself. 'They'll hang you for sure.'

'Thanks, mate.'

'By the way, what's Fiona McLeod like?'

'Great legs,' I said. 'Wonderful teeth.'

'Are you buying her to race or to breed?'

'How the hell would I know what she's like,' I said, exasperated. 'I haven't fronted up and introduced myself. I'm trying to be unobtrusive.'

'How? By chewing on a straw and talking out of the side of your mouth?'

'Yeah, and spitting in the dust.'

She asked me what I'd thought of Hamish McLeod.

'He's a pompous little prick. And vindictive. He's too pissweak to slug it out with Fiona, so he's hired me to grab the dogs.'

'Don't underestimate him,' Lizzie warned. 'Cowards can get very dangerous when they're cornered.'

'If he gives me a hard time, I'll bounce off his bald spot,' I said.

'And you'll end up in court,' she said. 'If he turns nasty, tell him Lizzie Darcy said hello, and does he remember the conference in Manila. 1983.'

'Tell me.'

She didn't. 'Only use it in an emergency. He might overreact.'

I stored that away and asked her what was going on in the real world.

'The usual. Faction fights, falling dollar, Liberal split, Labor out of touch with the people. Twenty million-dollar drug bust.'

Maybe Glen Innes wasn't so bad.

Before Lizzie rang off, she said: 'About the dogs. They're all god-fearing Scots up there, Syd; I'll bet they still go to church on Sundays.'

Of course.

Early on Sunday morning I returned to my possie on the highway and hunkered down to wait. I'd brought some stale ham sandwiches, Smith's chips, fruit cake and a big bottle of mango mineral water. At ten thirty I tortured myself with visions of scones and jam and cream and strong tea, and at lunch I had hallucinations about a baked dinner.

At a quarter to six the Woods' wagon appeared, heading for evening service: there were no dogs' noses pressed against the windows. Thank you, Lizzie Darcy, I thought; bless your little black convent girl's heart.

I drove to the farm and knocked, ready to trot out the lost traveller's tale, but the house was empty. Hysterical barking led me to the back yard where the dogs were chained up. At least I wouldn't be up for B & E. The dogs welcomed me with open paws. I could have stolen the whole farm for all they cared: they thought I'd come to take them for a walk. They were right.

The timing was perfect. There wasn't a flight to Sydney till the next afternoon. All going well, I'd be in Wahroonga before Fiona McLeod could hop a plane. I decided to go back the way I'd come: it was predictable, but I had a headstart.

After a certain amount of manic excitement, the dogs settled down and we barrelled along the New England Highway with a little help from the Beatles.

Outside Armidale I stopped at a big Golden Fleece for petrol and supplies and hamburger all round. The dogs turned up their noses, but hunger triumphed eventually. I bundled them back into the Valiant and waited in the shadows while the mechanic scraped the dead bugs off the windscreen. He was about thirty, compact and well-muscled, with tats and something wired about the eyes. A man with a short fuse.

As I watched, a teenage girl slipped out of the garage to talk to the dogs. She was a skinny, fox-faced little brunette wearing shorts, a tee shirt and a vivid black eye. I moved and she saw me and came over. A witness...

'Nice dogs,' she said.

'Yeah,' I said.

'What's their names?'

'Stan and Ollie.'

She frowned at me. 'Funny names.'

'Yeah,' I said. I didn't have the energy to explain Laurel and Hardy to a kid who probably thought *Police Academy* 6 was a masterpiece.

The mechanic went inside to get my change, and when he was out of earshot, she whispered urgently: 'Hey mister, how about giving me a lift?'

'Where to?'

'You're going to Sydney, aren't you?'

'Yeah.'

'That'll do. I can pay for some of the petrol.'

'No dice,' I said. This was an underage runaway who'd probably end up on the game in the Cross. And I'd end up on the front page of the *Mirror* with my coat over my head.

She started to snivel. 'Please. I gotta get away from Lance.'

'Is that Lance?'

'Yeah, he's me stepfather.'

'He give you the eye?'

She touched her cheek, blushed and nodded.

'I'm sorry, mate. It can't be done. I can't afford to have Lance after me at the moment. Or the cops.'

A mistake: her eyes popped open. The cops interested her; maybe I was an armed bandit. Anything was better than Lance, who shouted: 'Tracy! Get inside! I won't tell you again!'

Tracy scuttled away and I breathed again, then went into the men's to wash the stink of dogs and hamburgers off my hands. I was sorry for Tracy, but I couldn't save the whole suffering world. Not today anyway.

The dogs kept barking on the way out of Armidale till I lost my temper and shouted. They subsided immediately except for the occasional resentful yap: shock, no doubt. I put *Paris Texas* on the tape deck: this was definitely Ry Cooder country.

Then about two hundred kilometres down the highway Stan and Ollie started talking again with whiny growls ending in short barks. I decided they were trying to tell me something and pulled off the road for a comfort stop.

The dogs immediately erupted onto the grass, galloped away, stopped, sniffed round; then raced back, circling each other and barking. I could see why Fiona had refused to split them up. I was growing quite fond of the fools.

Getting bored, I whistled and they loped back and stood, panting up at me waiting for directions.

'In!' I said, pointing, and they hurled themselves into the back seat. There was a muffled grunt.

'OK,' I said. 'Get out.'

The old army blanket on the floor stirred, and a defiant face appeared. So this was what The Boys had been trying to tell me.

'Jesus, do you realise what you're doing to me? I could get ten years for this! You're a minor, for God's sake! I'm abducting a minor!'

My anger upset the dogs, who started up. 'Shut up, you stupid buggers!' I yelled. 'You're as bad as she is!'

The girl climbed out and made a small movement, as if to run, and I grabbed her arm. It was like holding a terrified sparrow. I stopped shouting, retracted my fangs and turned back into a human being. 'Get in the front,' I commanded. 'We're taking you home before the Highway Patrol catches up with me. Or bloody Lance.'

Tracy's old man might be waiting with a shotgun, Fiona McLeod might be thundering down the highway towards me, and we were probably the subject of a general dog alert, but I decided not to panic. Yet. With Tracy in the front and the dogs asleep in the back, I headed back to Armidale through the warm night to the sounds of the Beachboys.

At one point I caught Tracy looking at me suspiciously. 'It's not me,' I said. 'It's them.'

'Musta been Mum's hamburgers,' said Tracy, and we laughed. She wasn't such a bad kid, I decided.

My good vibrations ended abruptly at a roadblock near Uralla, where bits of a semi-trailer and a small sedan were scattered all over the road. The ambulances had gone but the police were still measuring skidmarks and talking to witnesses. Lights flashed and two-way radios blared.

The racket woke my passengers, and before I could move, Ollie squeezed through a window and bounded towards a policeman. Tracy started to open the door to go after him; I grabbed her and pushed her down in the seat.

'Do you want to get me arrested?' I hissed.

Ollie was showing off shamelessly to a young cop with a crewcut. Stan started to whine. 'Sit!' I ordered. He growled but obeyed.

'Stay here while I get the mutt,' I told Tracy.

'I'll make a deal with you,' she said.

'Talk,' I said. 'Fast. Before the deputy sheriff comes over for a chat.'

'I won't give you away if you put me on the Brisbane Express.'

'What the hell is the Brisbane Express?'

'It's a train. To Brisbane.'

'Where does it stop?'

'Coffs, Grafton, Casino, Kyogle,' she recited. She'd done this trip before. I looked up the map: the best bet was Grafton, up Highway 78. Hours away.

'Why Brisbane?' I asked, resigned.

'Me gran lives in Brisbane. She'll let me stay with her.'

The young policeman started towards me, with Ollie jumping all over him. 'Yes, yes! Anything!' I said, pushing Tracy onto the floor. I leapt out, smiling hard, and grabbed Ollie while the cop told me what a great dog he was.

'Get in the car before I boot you up the arse,' I snarled, and Ollie's tail stopped in mid wag. I waved cheerily and drove off, suppressing an urge to burn rubber.

For about twenty kilometres I harangued the girl. When I ran out of abuse she demanded equal time and I got her life story: there were no surprises.

We reached Grafton at dawn. A sleepy youth told us the train would be along at five nineteen, so we waited on the deserted platform eating Mars Bars. The dogs snoozed. I would have happily traded them for a coffee but the town was locked shut. We had strayed off the map into the twilight zone.

Then a couple of ghostly backpackers appeared out of the gloom and the train arrived. I said goodbye to Tracy and gave her a hundred dollars and told her not to spend it all in one place.

'Will you be safe on the train?'

'God, you're ridiculous,' she said. 'I'm fifteen!'

'Send me a postcard, then. So I'll know you're OK.'

I started to walk away.

'Syd!' said Tracy. I turned around. 'Syd, I wouldn't...' her voice broke. 'I wouldn't have dobbed you really, you know.'

I held up my hands: 'Please, I don't want to hear this!'

I whistled the dogs, but they refused to budge: they didn't want to be left alone with me. Finally Tracy shouted: 'Go on! Git!' and they gave up and came quietly.

I saw her face at the train window as it pulled out, just a forlorn grubby kid with no future. She waved, I waved, the dogs barked. We set off for Sydney again.

On the way back I rang McLeod's office and told him to meet me at a picnic spot in Kuring-gai Chase to hand over the dogs.

I found McLeod's BMW in the parking lot and pulled in beside him. As I was getting out of the car, a white Mercedes convertible glided in behind us and cut off our escape route. Fiona McLeod and a good looking man climbed out and walked towards me. Goodbye bonus and goodbye Lucy Le Gay, I thought. The dogs went mad.

Fiona was smiling. The man was not. He looked dissipated up close, and the hazel eyes were cold and empty, but I lost interest in his face when I saw the shotgun in his hands. There goes the neighbourhood, I thought. He pointed it nonchalantly at my belly.

Catching the expression on my face, the man smiled. I liked him better the other way.

'My brother Ambrose,' said Fiona politely.

Ambrose said softly: 'The dogs.'

Fiona opened the door and the dogs spilled out rapturously and leapt all over her. She gave me a dirty look and said: 'What on earth have you been feeding them?'

When she had them safely stowed in the Mercedes, Ambrose lowered the gun and said: 'Try not to get in my way again, sweetheart.' He looked in McLeod's direction and spat on the ground.

Then they drove off, looking like an ordinary yuppie family in a car ad. Stan and Ollie didn't give me as much as a backward glance.

I'd been concentrating too hard to register fear, but now my knees started to shake. As soon as the coast was clear, Hamish McLeod surfaced, pale and sweating.

'Thanks a lot,' I said.

'He wouldn't have shot you,' he said, without conviction.

My fear turned to rage: 'Look, give me my money and let me get out of here before I tear your cheeks off, fatface!'

We glared at each other and I got into the front seat of his car.

'What happened?' he asked, writing my cheque.

'I used my judgment,' I said.

There was no bonus on the cheque. I looked at him inquiringly.

'You didn't get the dogs back safely,' he said. 'That was our deal.'

You had to admire a man whose greed was stronger than his sense of self-preservation.

'The deal didn't have any gun-toting brothers-in-law in it, McLeod,' I said. 'Let's just call it danger money.'

His face set and he folded his arms, looking like an obstinate canetoad.

I held the cheque aloft and said mildly: 'By the way, I have this really good friend, Lizzie Darcy. I believe you've met?'

I'd captured his attention at last. 'She said to say hi. She said you'd remember her.'

I tore up the cheque. 'Manila. 1983.'

He seemed to deflate in front of my eyes, and the pen fell from his fingers. I picked it up and placed it in his hand and he wrote me another cheque mechanically.

I cashed it as soon as I got to Darlinghurst, then called Lizzie and told her I'd had to play the Manila card.

'Old Ambrose back in town, eh?' said Lizzie. 'I'd heard they started a cleanup in Manila. Sydney's in for a crime wave. I'd stay out of his way if I were you, Syd.'

'Yeah, that's what he said. The least you can do is tell me what it's all about.'

'You might need it now you've come to Ambrose's attention,' she agreed. 'I was covering an international banking conference. McLeod and some of the boys had a party in a hotel room and it got a little rough and one of the local working girls did a dive off the balcony.

'It was all hushed up. I'm pretty sure Ambrose fixed it for McLeod. He was running a joint in Mabini Street at the time: it was probably one of his girls.'

'A close-knit family,' I observed.

'Ambrose is pretty loathesome, but he seems to be genuinely fond of his sister.'

'Does she know about what happened in Manila?'

'If she didn't already know, I think she probably copped an earful yesterday, don't you?'

'Nice bargaining chip in a divorce settlement,' I said.

'Couldn't happen to a nicer man. But maybe they deserve each other. What do you think of the toothsome Fiona now?'

'Beats me,' I said. 'Some of her friends would go all the way for her, but she married a slug and her brother is a pimp.'

'And she goes to church,' said Lizzie. 'Very complex.'

A couple of days later I got a postcard with the Big Pineapple on it. Tracy thanked me and invited me to visit Queensland any time.

Maybe it was all worth it, I thought sentimentally. Then I saw the last sentence. 'PS. Your as weak as piss Sid.'

SEMI-PRECIOUS

'May you live in interesting times' is said to be a Chinese curse. If anyone had the ability to hex me, it would be Grace Ho. Her breathy voice on the phone asking me to drop by her apartment urgently affected me like a kick in the gut.

'What for?' I asked. The last time we'd met, Grace had led me around by the nose, leaving it decidedly out of joint. Nothing was ever straight-forward with this lady: I'd need more information before I'd volunteer for another bout.

'It is a family matter, Mr Fish. I need your help.'

Grace was devious and totally unscrupulous: her idea of help was sure to be flexible and probably dangerous. But she was also beautiful and oddly fascinating and I was flattered. I went.

The apartment looked the same — polished floors, Chinese rugs, Italian leather, expensive harbour views — except for some new Papunya paintings.

'Very nice,' I said, inspecting them. 'You're interested in Aboriginal art, Ms Ho?'

'Of course, Mr Fish. And they have already appreciated considerably.'

Some things never change.

Before getting down to business, Grace made coffee in an Italian infuser and plied me with French pastries. The last time I'd been here I'd got Chinese tea and insults. I started to worry.

When the story came out, it concerned Precious, Grace's fifteen-year-old sister, who had gone missing three days earlier between Elizabeth Bay and St Clotilde's, an expensive boarding school in

Rose Bay. I asked Grace to tell me about Precious: was she the sort of girl who would run away?

'My sister has been very well brought up,' said Grace. I've sent her to the best schools.'

Which was one way of refusing to answer the question: if Precious were less than perfect, Grace wasn't going to be the one to tell me.

'What does she look like?' I asked.

'Chinese,' said Grace and looked at me from under her lashes, but she disappeared and returned with a silver-framed portrait of her sister. Precious was a younger version of Grace, delicate as an ivory carving, but with a fuck-you look about the mouth and eyes.

'Very pretty,' I said, 'How much money did she have on her?'

'Only fifty dollars. I pay her allowance into an account each month.'

Either Little Sister couldn't be trusted with large amounts of money or Grace was trying to instil the work ethic into the girl. Judging by that face, I didn't like her chances.

I asked Grace who Precious' friends were, but she was vague. Some girls from school, she thought. Boyfriends?

'She is very young, Mr Fish. I only allow her to go out in groups.'

Who was Grace kidding? Precious looked to me like she'd been climbing out of dormitory windows since she was twelve.

I thought I should start at the school but Grace refused. The headmistress had been told Precious was suffering a nervous collapse, and Grace still had ideas about sending the girl back to St Clotilde's if she turned up safe, sound and scandal-free.

I couldn't do the job with both hands tied behind my back, so I disregarded my client's wishes. Posing as a doctor wanting to consult the girl's teachers about her mental state, I rang the school. My pompous medical manner impressed the school secretary but didn't get me through to the headmistress. Instead I was passed on to one of the teachers, Joan Brooks.

Ms Brooks was gracious until I mentioned Precious' name. Though I probed as gently as a Macquarie Street gynaecologist, Ms Brooks seemed oddly reluctant to talk about the girl.

After stoking up on coffee and a cheese Danish, I called Lizzie for a yarn and told her I was looking for Grace Ho's sister. Lizzie has looked under most of the tiles in Sydney's cultural mosaic: she knew Grace through interviewing Devon Kent, and had a healthy respect for her.

'How come you're working for That Woman?' she demanded.

'She asked me.'

'Don't pussyfoot with me. You know what I mean. You know where her money comes from.'

'Look, I'm not delivering parcels for her,' I protested. 'I'm looking for a runaway kid.'

There was a silence, then Lizzie said: 'You know what I think? I think you're mesmerised by her. Just be careful, that's all: Grace eats big dopes like you for breakfast.'

The shot went home. I was a sucker for Grace; I admired her cool perfection, her ruthlessness and her ability to look after herself in the nasty and brutish world of drug dealing. And Grace had a human side — she'd remained loyal to Devon Kent when the rest of the pack were baying for her blood.

'You're just jealous,' I said feebly.

'No. I'm concerned about you. Watch out for Grace and her friends. They play for keeps.'

Despite her misgivings, Lizzie didn't let me down. She had a spy in every network in Sydney; this time it was a friend with a daughter at St Clotilde's.

'Precious is apparently a genius at passive resistance,' Lizzie told me when she rang back a couple of hours later. 'Does exactly as she likes. She also looks like a doll and has beautiful clothes and fast men friends. The other girls hate her, of course. She probably makes them look like clodhoppers.'

It was something, but not enough to tell me whether or not the girl had gone off under her own steam.

Help came from an unexpected quarter when I got a phone call from Joan Brooks, who had succumbed either to conscience or the desire to chance her luck with a medical man.

We met at the Lord Dudley in Woollahra. I was expecting Doris Day to walk in but Joan Brooks looked more like Lana Turner—

cool, blond and curvy under her executive suit. I was so overcome I stood up. She put out her hand. I wondered if I were supposed to kiss it, but compromised by giving it a sort of squeeze. She almost frowned.

To atone, I ordered champagne from the barman, who had trouble unriveting his gaze from her crisp, white blouse long enough to get the cork out of the bottle. We exchanged pleasantries, and she said suddenly: 'You're not a doctor. Who are you?'

She was curious rather than hostile, so I said: 'And you're not Doris Day.' This time she did frown.

'Can you respect a confidence?'

'If it's disgusting enough,' she said, and I decided our Ms Brooks was all right.

'I'm working for Grace Ho,' I explained. 'Precious has been mislaid...'

'That's a change,' she interrupted.

'... between Elizabeth Bay and the school,' I went on. 'Grace is keen to get her back, preferably without alerting New South Wales's finest, and definitely without Derryn Hinch in tow.'

Joan Brooks thought Precious' disappearance was probably just a lost weekend. 'There's no real need for Precious to bolt now. The school has never seriously cramped her style, and she's leaving at the end of the year anyway.'

'What's she like?' I asked.

'Uncontrollable. If Grace Ho didn't have a very strong investment in the school building fund, Precious would be at the local state high school by now. If they'd take her.'

'Is she that bad?'

'The girl is as bent as Grace, but she's a nymphomaniac as well.'

'You don't like her,' I deadpanned.

She laughed. 'That's not entirely true. She's a bad influence in the school but she's more interesting than most of the ladies we turn out. And she certainly has the courage of her convictions.'

'Which are?'

'Good drugs, bad men and other people's money.'

'Sounds sensible to me,' I said. 'Do you think she's got into the sort of company that might go in for kidnapping?'

That opened her eyes. 'Is that what you're thinking?'

I said I was reserving judgment until I'd checked out Precious' boyfriends.

'I can't help you there,' she said, standing up to go. 'Excuse me, I have to go: I've got a meeting.'

'Give me a call if you remember anything,' I said, without much hope.

'Just one thing,' she said. 'If it is a kidnapping, they're in for a rough time. They'll be in touch soon begging Grace to take her back.'

My card disappeared into her handbag and she exited in a cloud of expensive scent. For a moment I almost wished I were a doctor; then I remembered some of the ones I'd seen on the news.

The mention of kidnapping had apparently alarmed Ms Brooks, and she rang next day and advised me to talk to Eva Nagy, Precious' best friend at St Clotilde's. I asked her to set it up for me.

I caught up with the girl in the Cosmopolitan at Double Bay, amid the shrill babble of overdressed women, overtanned social climbers and men with gold chains and no visible means of support. Eva Nagy was fifteen going on twenty-eight, olive skinned, gold braceleted, languid, sultry. Long brown eyes and Magyar cheekbones completed the trap. I pitied the school.

She ordered Irish coffee and watched me carefully for a reaction. I didn't have one. Then she gave me lots of eye business over the top of her glass. I wasn't in the running for a law suit and didn't respond, but it gave me a flash of how dangerous Eva and Precious would be together, on the prowl.

I told the girl that Grace had hired me to find Precious, and asked where her friend might have gone. And with whom.

'Why should I tell you anything?' she asked, smiling sweetly and opening her eyes wide in a doomed attempt to appear innocent.

'Because something might have happened to her.'

'Precious can look after herself,' she answered, burying her nose in whipped cream.

I tried another tack. 'The way I see it, you've got no choice. You cough up, or Grace Ho will pay a visit to your Dad and fill him in on your extra-curricular activities.'

Peter Nagy was a pillar of the Jewish community — B'Nai B'rith, sponsor of the Australian Opera, Friend of the Art Gallery, golf-partner of politicians. Who knows, he may even have been nominated for father of the year: stranger choices have been made.

The girl's eyes widened slightly, then narrowed. Fear is definitely uncool.

'OK,' she said. 'If she's skipped, she'll be with Renzo Gambino.'

Christ, I thought, not L'Onorata Societa. 'Who's he?'

'His father owns Gambino Seafoods. Loads of money...'

'I'm not interested in his father. Where do I find Renzo? What does he do?'

'Nothing. He's supposed to be doing Law at Sydney Uni but he just hangs out most of the time.'

'Where?'

'Whale Beach. They've got a shack up there.'

I got the address, paid for the drinks and thanked her. As she was getting into a taxi, she turned and said with a smile: 'Tell Grace to go bite her arse.'

That made me laugh: I like a bad loser. Eva's father was wasting twelve grand a year trying to turn her into a lady. I didn't mind: personally I prefer women.

I thrashed the Valiant out to Whale Beach, round the gleaming cliffs, through the bastions of privilege, past expensive boutiques, specialty shops and liquor stores. I found the beach house easily and parked the car. Nobody answered my knock, so I walked round the side. Immediately a head bobbed up above the fence, and I was bailed up by a codger with a straw hat, bermuda shorts and the undemocratic air of a retired company director.

I didn't think he'd believe I was the Avon lady, so I told him I was looking for Renzo Gambino. His mouth turned down; Renzo obviously lowered the tone of the neighbourhood.

'Him!' he barked. 'What for? Has he held up a bank or something?'

'Not that I know of. I'm trying to locate a lady friend of his.'

'Which one?' he asked. 'It's like a motel here. They come and go all the time.'

'A Chinese girl. A very young one.'

'You must mean Shanghai Lil,' he said. 'But she didn't look all that young to me.'

'She's fifteen.'

He was shocked: his fantasies had been illegal. 'I haven't seen her for a couple of weeks. Renzo either.'

He sounded disappointed: Renzo's love life was a lot more interesting than exterminating thrips.

'Got any idea where he might have gone?'

'The family owns a unit at the Gold Coast, but I don't know where.'

As I pushed open the front gate a red Ferrari pulled in with a scream of tyres. Two young Italians got out and waited for me. They were togged out in the latest Milan copies from Najee and I could smell their aftershave on the sea breeze. They were between me and my car.

'You a friend of Gambino's?' demanded the shorter of the two. The other cracked his knuckles like a comic-strip villain.

'No.'

'Wha chew doin here then?'

'Private Investigator,' I said. 'Looking for a girl.'

'Gino, he's got plenty a girls,' joked the second banana, and his boss scowled at him.

'Which girl?' he insisted.

'None of your business,' I said, getting tired of their macho shit.

Gino said something in Italian, and his amico started to circle round the back of me. I measured the distance to the car and decided I wouldn't make it. I was glad I didn't carry a gun; the temptation to shoot morons like this would be overpowering.

The posse closed in. There was no way I could beat both of them, but I was going to enjoy landing a couple of punches on their pretty, vicious mugs. Suddenly they froze. It couldn't have been my tough expression that frightened them, so I looked behind me. The cavalry had arrived. The old bloke was standing at the fence pointing a hunting rifle at them.

'Out!' he ordered.

Eyes glued to the gun, they conferred in Italian, told me they wouldn't forget my face, and roared off, shattering the suburban stillness.

'Thanks,' I said.

'Don't thank me, I enjoyed it,' he said. 'Don't like Italians.

Came across a lot of them in the war. In the desert, you know. No discipline.'

Back in town I dropped in on Grace to see if she wanted me to check out the Gambino's Surfers Paradise flat. I was hoping she'd let me go north so I could look up Katy Kincaid: it was not to be.

'I know where Precious is, Mr Fish,' said Grace. 'And I am confident that I can get her back safely without help.'

'Where is she?'

'I am not at liberty to divulge that, Mr Fish.'

'So I'm off the case.'

'Yes. You have been most helpful.'

She wrote me a cheque and led me to the door. Her expression hadn't changed, but there was a new tension in her. By observing Grace closely, I'd discovered there were degrees of inscrutability. Nowadays I could detect little signs that clued me into what was going on in her head. She was worried.

It looked to me like somebody had snatched Precious and was putting the bite on Grace, but if she didn't want help, there was nothing I could do. I was out of the game.

But not for long. Three days later I got a curt message from Grace asking me to see her.

After we'd exchanged the ritual courtesies, she said: 'I've received some information, Mr Fish...'

'Don't you think it's time we got down to first names, Grace?' I interrupted.

'I've received some information, Sydney,' said Grace, not missing a beat. 'It seems Precious is living in an apartment in the Connaught owned by Mr Raymond Ling.'

'You mean Precious is shacked up with Raymond Ling? Raymond Ling who owns the restaurants and is very married to the lovely Monique, queen of the social columns?'

'You are not taking this seriously, Sydney.'

'Sure I am. In fact, I'll get right on the phone and tell Raymond Ling if he doesn't get your sister back here within the hour, we'll call the police. She is under age, you know.'

I walked towards the phone. Grace slid up behind me and restrained me with iron claws.

'Please, Sydney. It is not so simple.'

I'd thought not.

Grace sat down, smoothed leather over perfect thighs and said: 'Precious did not initially join Mr Ling voluntarily, you see. There was a small misunderstanding between Mr Ling and myself...'

'Over money, by any chance?'

'Over money. Mr Ling thought that removing Precious might encourage me to close negotiations speedily.'

'He kidnapped her?'

'Yes.'

'And you couldn't very well go to the police in case they wanted to know the details of your business with Mr Ling.'

'You can understand my position, Sydney.'

'Have you agreed to Ling's terms?'

'I was seriously considering doing so, when I was informed that Mr Ling has become attached to my sister, and had even spoken of leaving his family to be with her.'

'Looking on the bright side, that means he's not likely to kill her to get his money.'

'No. But it seems that Precious returns Mr Ling's regard and has formed an alliance with him.'

Ms Brooks had turned out to be a good judge of character. 'She's gone over to the other side?'

'Yes. I want her back.'

'So you can strangle her?'

'That won't be necessary. But an extended stay in a Swiss finishing school might improve her judgment considerably, don't you think, Sydney?'

I was astonished: Grace Ho had almost cracked a joke.

'Who knows about this little disagreement you're having with Ling?' I asked.

Grace lowered her eyes. 'Just the two of us. The object of the disagreement was a small, private transaction...'

So Grace and Raymond Ling had been doing deals without the knowledge of the syndicate. Grace wanted to grow old gracefully, enjoy her ill-gotten gains in peace and perhaps even get an Order of Australia for her philanthropic work for Chinese senior citizens;

that meant I had to get Precious back from Ling without going public and revealing why he'd snatched her.

'Do you trust me to take on Raymond Ling? I asked.

Grace nodded. She didn't have a lot of choice. The Ho family were already creating enough havoc in Chinatown without Grace beating down the door of Raymond Ling's love nest. We agreed she would stick close to the phone, prostrate with worry.

I had no idea how to proceed, but at least for the time being the odds were favourable. With Ling isolated from the syndicate, it was one on one.

I decided to see if Lizzie could come up with any ideas—she'd written extensively on the Chinese community. Over yum cha at the Chinatown Gardens restaurant, I filled her in on Raymond Ling and Precious.

'He's mad,' she said.

'You haven't seen her picture,' I said. 'I'd say he's lucky.'

'For the moment. Monique will make his life hell, her family will start plotting to take his kids away, and eventually Precious will get sick of living with an old fart who spends too much time in his restaurants. Then the fun will start.'

'In the meantime, he's probably having a ball.'

'Yeah, till she wears him out. These old blokes are much more interested in the idea of sex than actually doing lots of it. They just don't have the stamina.'

'You'd know,' I said unkindly.

Lizzie was dating a politician who'd been married twice and had grandchildren.

'Thanks,' she said.

'How is Reg?'

'Busy. But then, he's a very important man.' Her tone told me she was going off Reg. I cheered up. We grinned at each other. I know she'll never have me but that doesn't stop me getting pissed off when she falls in love.

When I asked Lizzie about Chinatown politics, she told me a story. 'I went to a banquet in Chinatown once. For travel writers. Hosted by the Dixon Street Friendship Association or something like that.'

'Sounds like a CIA front. And since when have you been a travel writer?'

'Since I needed a free trip to New York.'

That must have been when she was having a glamorous international affair with a *Time Magazine* staffer. She told me she'd broken it off finally because she couldn't stand his prose style. But I digress.

'The food was terrible, of course,' she went on, 'but the whole thing was irresistibly weird. Towards the end this old Chinese gentleman came in with his entourage. He was the president of the association.'

'So?'

'So he was quite sinister, obviously some sort of Mr Big down here: the owner and the Chinese waiters were terrified of him. He didn't speak a word of English, and he had this slick, bilingual lawyer translating for him. The lawyer reminded me of the Godfather, with whatshisface playing the Harvard-educated mouthpiece...'

'Robert Duval,' I said. 'Are you sure you weren't hallucinating from too much cheap plonk and MSG?'

'Yeah, the wine was awful... But seriously...'

'What's the bloody punchline?' I asked. 'You're burying the lead!'

'So now you're giving me lessons in journalism? My point is this. The Chinese are paranoid about bad publicity. They absolutely freaked a couple of years ago when Madame Lu got charged with trafficking from her restaurant down here'.

'If Precious is cutting a swathe through Raymond Ling's marriage and causing a feud between the Lings and the Chows—they're Monique's clan—maybe the boss would like to know about it before it gets violent and ends up on page one of the *Herald*.'

'So somebody should tell him,' I said faintly.

'Yeah, somebody should,' said Lizzie. She scrabbled around in her wallet and came up with a business card, held it up and smiled nastily: 'Maybe someone should call Robert Duval'.

I was trapped. I took the card. Robert Duval, it seemed, was being played by Dr Stanley Wu.

There was something subtly different about Lizzie today, I realised on the down escalator, so I quizzed her about it.

'I've shaved off my moustache,' she said.

'No, really. Have you done something to your hair?'

'If you must know, I bought myself some sexy underwear.'

'The sisterhood won't like that. I thought feminists were only allowed to wear Bonds Cottontails. White ones.'

'Well, I caught sight of myself back on in DJ's changeroom and got so depressed I went straight out and spent three hundred dollars on this stuff.'

Whereupon, to the astonishment and delight of a bent Chinese great-grandfather, she executed a perfect No Knickers manoeuvre to reveal black stockings, suspender belt and lace panties.

As we wove off, laughing, to find a cab, I said: 'Go easy on Reg, or you'll be up on a manslaughter charge.'

It would take leverage to get me in to see Dr Wu, so I contacted Wayne Wong, who'd grown up with me in a tough, inner-city neighbourhood. Wayne and I had traded insults, punches, marbles, and finally a few confidences, and had kept in touch sporadically over the years.

Wayne had come from a hard-up, hard-working Chinese family, but he was impatient to grab his share of the Australian dream and had been a conman since kindergarten. He was still mixed up in every scam going. These days Wayne did PR for the Australia-Chinese Society—officially, anyway: actually he was the conduit for the Chinese community's donations to political parties. In certain circles he'd be called a lobbyist.

Bilingual and ingratiating, Wayne had bartered his talents for a big house at Randwick, a lovely blond Aussie wife, two little Wongs learning the violin at Sydney Grammar, a Mercedes Benz and a Volvo station wagon, and lately—if my sources at the Paddo-Woollahra RSL were to be believed—a Chinese girlfriend.

When we met for lunch at Mario's, Wayne was wearing an expensive shiny suit and a heavy gold watch.

'Doing well, I see,' I commented. 'Business good?'

'A PR man's life is never easy.'

I snorted. 'Save the bullshit for Boucher, Wayne; I need a favour.'

'I dunno, mate....'

'Wait till you hear what it is, sweetheart. You might find you want to help me.'

'So what do you want, Sydney?' he asked, resigned, lighting a cigarette with a flashy lighter.

'I need to talk to Stanley Wu.'

The lighter stopped in mid-air. 'Dr Wu? You want to see Dr Wu? What the fuck for, if I might be permitted to ask?'

'I want to insert some information into certain channels.'

'What channels?'

'I want to let somebody very important know that Monique Ling is very unhappy about the fact that her husband has taken a concubine.'

'Christ! Are you working for Monique Ling?'

'No, I'm working for the concubine's Big Sister, Grace Ho.'

He whistled. 'And you're caught between Grace Ho and Raymond Ling. Sydney, I hope you've got excellent life insurance. Count me out.'

'Before you make up your mind, Wayne,' I said with a shit-eating grin, 'How's Pat?'

'Pat's fine,' he said suspiciously.

'And the kids?'

'The kids are great.'

'That's good. I thought maybe Pat was upset.'

'About what?'

'About what you do on Thursday nights when she thinks you're out at Macquarie studying law.'

'You arsehole!'

'Wayne, all I want is an introduction to Dr Wu. You're an influential member of the Chinese community, I'm sure you can find a way.'

I called a waiter and paid the bill. It was the least I could do, and Grace was picking up the tab anyway. Wayne sat on, staring into his chardonnay-semillon. 'Call me when you've got a meet, mate,' I said. 'And give my love to Pat.'

Satisfied that he would come good, I rang Grace and told her it was time Monique Ling found out about her rival. If by some extraordinary chance she didn't know already.

'Is that a good idea, Sydney?'

I said yes and told her why. 'We're going to use a little Chinese psychology here, Grace. If we can sic Monique onto Raymond Ling and get her family fighting his, the whole of Chinatown will take sides. Unless I miss my guess, there are lots of powerful people who don't want dirty Chinese laundry washed in public. I think they might bring a little pressure to bear to have Precious returned to her loving sister.'

Grace laughed. 'It's good. I wish I had thought of it myself.'

High praise indeed.

Chinatown was jumping, spilling over with investment money fleeing Hong Kong. The din of construction drowned out the babble of Chinese shoppers and tourists as high rises with three floors of eateries went up in the ashes of small family restaurants. It was hard to tell what the ancients sunning themselves like lizards on the benches in Dixon Street thought of it all: perhaps they were dreaming of their ancestral villages in China.

Dr Wu was tall, thin and reptilian, with an excellent grasp of English and eyes as cold as pebbles in a Manchurian stream. He made it clear I was keeping him from important matters, and was polite in a way that gives courtesy a bad name.

An appreciable silence followed my inquiries about the welfare of Precious Ho.

'What makes you think, Mr Fish, that I would be remotely interested in the whereabouts of a runaway schoolgirl? Or that I would even recognise her if I saw her? After all, we know all Chinese look alike.'

This was supposed to make me feel like round-eyed racist but I persevered. I don't like being typecast. 'Now tell me you wouldn't recognise Grace Ho if you fell over her in Hay Street,' I said.

He laughed quietly. It was more chilling than his politeness. 'Of course I'm acquainted with Miss Ho,' he said. 'She is very well known in Chinatown for her beauty and business acumen.'

'Ms Ho is very concerned for the welfare of her sister, Dr Wu; I understand family is very important to the Chinese. At the same time, she is concerned not to attract attention to her family troubles. However, if Precious is not found soon, I can't guarantee her continued patience.'

Either the appeal to the Chinese family code worked, or the veiled threat of going public planted the tiniest bamboo shoot of doubt.

'Please let Miss Ho know, from me, that I will give the matter my closest consideration, Mr Fish.'

It sounded like a letter from the Department of Administrative Affairs, but then the Chinese love bureaucracy almost as much as they love gambling, and seem to be better at it. The interview was terminated.

I'd done all I could for the time being, so I rang Grace with a progress report. She was impressed that I'd got in to see Dr Wu; he was known to be a very private man.

'What do you suggest we do now, Sydney?'

'Sit back and wait. Though you might wish to stir the pot a little.'

That gave me an idea. I rang my favourite Chinese takeaway and ordered spare ribs with plum sauce, crispy skin chicken and boiled rice. I decided against vegetables: I didn't want to ruin my reputation. Then I ate it with two bottles of Balmain Bock in front of the TV, watching Clive Robertson subverting the news.

Grace rang next day to tell me Precious was free, apparently none the worse for wear. 'And Mr Ling has decided to stay with his loving wife and family.'

'And Precious has agreed to go back to school?'

'Well... uh?'

'Come on, Grace: she either has or she hasn't.'

There was a pause while Grace decided how to package the information. 'Precious is not here, Sydney. She's gone to Surfer's Paradise.'

'You sent her to Surfers?'

'Not exactly. She went straight from the Connaught to Surfers Paradise.'

The penny dropped. 'She's skipped again.'

'Yes.'

'But why Surfer's?'

'It appears she's travelling with someone called Renzo Gambino, who owns an apartment there.'

'So do you want me to go after her?'

The long silence that ensued gave me time to do some sums and figure out why Grace wasn't hot-footing it to the Gold Coast. By merging her networks and money and the Gambino deep sea fishing fleet, Grace could cut loose from the syndicate and set up shop for herself. A triumph for multiculturalism: a marriage made in heaven.

I must have been thinking aloud, because Grace's slightly surprised voice cut across my calculations.

'Why, thank you, Sydney, I'm sure they will be very happy together.'

Fish Sauce

I usually avoid rich old women; they have too little to lose.

So when Barbara Brabazon rang and said she wanted to see me, I had mixed feelings. Like everyone else, I'd read that her only son Jack, a Federal Liberal MP, had been found dead of a heart attack in his car in one of Sydney's western suburbs, and like almost everyone else, I wasn't prostrate with grief.

That heart attack had probably cost Brabazon's mother a cool million, with forty-two years of grooming, scheming and deals down the drain. She was fighting off despair the only way she knew — denial.

At forty two, Brabazon was still promising: he'd been around long enough to become a household name, but not long enough to bore the householders to death. He'd made a career of sorts out of being a Vietnam veteran, and had ended up something of an expert on South-East Asian politics and Liberal Party spokesman on the subject. When the Liberals had gone into Opposition, he'd become Shadow Minister for Foreign Affairs for a time.

In the Agent Orange debate, he'd taken up the vets' case against the Labor Government, but that was probably politics as much as conviction; he'd never been overburdened with principles.

I'd met Brabazon around the traps when I flacked for Barry Cromer, and had found him self-consciously weighty, overcompensating perhaps for his playboy good looks and silvertail background. But then, wealth seems to cause personality damage in all but saints and Quaker philanthropists.

All in all, Brabazon had enjoyed a dream run. Ordinary folks tend to dislike men like him, even as they grovel and defer. I'm no exception.

The dowager Brabazon had a reputation for coming on like the Red Queen, and suffered from selective amnesia about names and faces. I wondered who'd jolted her memory about me; perhaps she'd filed me under unsavoury but useful. She received me in her Point Piper living room, all stiff upper lip and excellent tweed. A put-upon Mediterranean maid served us weak tea with lemon and some fruitcake so dry it must have come from Miss Havisham's wedding feast.

After I'd paid sufficient homage to the memory of the crown prince, Barbara Brabazon got to the point. 'I'm not satisfied with the police investigation. I want you to find out what Jack was doing in Strathfield.'

'Doesn't his wife know?' I asked.

'Deborah is very distressed,' she answered, with the care of a pointsman in a mine field. 'She's keen to put this behind her. She accepts that Jack died accidentally and doesn't believe re-opening the investigation would serve any purpose.'

It sounded suspiciously like a press release, and was just as credible.

'But you don't think it was a natural death?'

'I don't know. I just feel there's something wrong about it. At the very least, I want to know where my son spent the last hours of his life.'

'Even if it might be a little... embarrassing?' I was implying that her son might have departed this world in the arms of an over-enthusiastic mistress: he wouldn't be the first in Australian politics.

'I'm an old woman, Mr Fish. I've seen a lot of life. I haven't liked all of it, but none of it has killed me so far. I want to know — whatever you find out.'

On the way back to my office in Darlinghurst, I stopped off at a library and read all the newspaper accounts of Brabazon's death, and when I got in, made a phone call to Liberal Party headquarters in Woolloomooloo. Then I rang Deborah Brabazon and made an appointment to see her at their Turramurra house.

I didn't know much about Jack Brabazon's wife, who kept a very low profile. She turned out to be tall and brown haired, with cool, played-down good looks. She was the sort of woman men like to think they could awaken with the right touch. Staring into those hazel eyes, I decided they'd be wrong.

I said her mother-in-law had hired me to look into her husband's death.

'He died of a heart attack,' she said. 'What more does she need to know?'

'She feels there is something odd... unfinished about it.'

'When a young man dies there has to be something unfinished about it,' she said. 'But it's not necessarily odd.'

There was obviously little warmth between the Brabazon women. Their open rivalry must have complicated Brabazon's life, but who knows, he may have enjoyed the power.

'So you don't think there was anything significant about your husband dying alone, late at night in the western suburbs?'

'He was obviously on his way home from somewhere,' she said. 'And anyway, everybody dies alone.'

I didn't allow myself to be diverted by philosophising. 'But you haven't any explanation for him being in Strathfield?'

'No.'

This was tougher than running up a down escalator.

'No ideas?'

She sighed. 'It could have been political work.'

'I know he didn't address any of the party faithful that night, Mrs Brabazon. I checked: there weren't any meetings on out there.'

She turned her palms up; the gesture said she didn't know. Perhaps she didn't care.

I'd hit a brick wall, and wondered why. It had to have something to do with the Brabazon marriage, which had reputedly been made in smoky backrooms rather than in heaven. Deborah's father, George White, had controlled the New South Wales Liberal machine for decades, and Jack Brabazon's marriage had guaranteed the younger man preselection for a safe seat. Barbara Brabazon supplied the money, Jack the ambition, Deborah the connections — an unbeatable team. Or was it?

I told the widow I'd keep her posted on developments but I was talking to her back. She was hugging herself and staring out the window. I let myself out. No maids here.

A phone call from Barbara Brabazon to the Commissioner of Police got me in to talk to the cop who'd investigated the death.

Detective Inspector Col Patterson was a long streak with a well-honed clodhopper routine designed to lull the punters into a false sense of security. He retained some of the bushman's dry self-deprecation, but had acquired plenty of city savvy over the years on the Homicide Squad. Patterson could change from a likeable hick to a hard man faster than the flash of a rubber truncheon. He was complex and devious, and though his mind sometimes moved slowly, it ground exceedingly fine.

I'd run up against Patterson while working for a foot-in-the-door television program, and he'd scorched the hairs off my ears over an interview I'd done with one of his witnesses. He recognised me and his eyes narrowed but he couldn't remember my name: it was a joke in the department that if Patterson remembered the name of the deceased in a case, the investigation had gone on too long.

He told me the police had found no evidence of foul play; Brabazon had died of a heart attack.

'In the car?'

'As far as we know.'

He put his hands in his pockets and leaned back in his chair: 'What's on Mrs Brabazon's mind? Was Brabazon up to something?'

I said I didn't know, but that I thought she was relying on intuition rather than evidence.

The look he shot me spoke volumes about his opinion of women's intuition. 'Strange bloke, Brabazon. Why do you suppose a man like that would be so interested in Vietnam?'

'Nostalgia?' I suggested, waiting for the punchline. Patterson was playing me like a trout.

'Kept up his contacts with the Vietnamese community in Australia, did he?' he probed.

'Yeah. He made a career out of them. And he was a big shot in the Vietnam Veterans' Association.'

'Well, you might start with his Vietnamese friends,' said Patterson. 'He'd been eating Vietnamese food just before he died.'

I thanked him and got up to leave.

'So you're a PI, now...'

'Syd,' I prompted.

'That's right; Syd. Sydney Fish. Going up in the world, Sydney?' All this with a perfectly straight face.

I shouted myself some rather tired roast pork in the police canteen, then withdrew to Darlinghurst to check my messages: nothing, apart from a polite suggestion that I ring my bank manager, no doubt about my overdraft. He had Buckley's, unless I solved the mystery of the politician's death, and that meant finding out where Brabazon had eaten his last *ga xao lan*.

There were probably three hundred Vietnamese restaurants in Greater Sydney. Overcome with indigestion and the immensity of the task, I procrastinated and called Lizzie Darcy.

'What's happening, Syd?'

'I've gotta find out where Jack Brabazon ate his last supper,' I said.

Lizzie's antennae twanged. 'Why? Was he poisoned?'

'Heart attack,' I said. 'But the dowager Brabazon suspects foul play.'

'Why?'

'Because he was found in his car in Strathfield, and nobody can think of a good reason why he was out there.'

'It might be something simple, like a girlfriend,' suggested Lizzie.

'Maybe a Vietnamese girlfriend,' I said.

'Vietnamese?'

'Yeah, he ate Vietnamese food just before he died.'

'Strathfield is on the way to Cabramatta,' said Lizzie, closing in fast. Cabramatta is the biggest Vietnamese ghetto in New South Wales, so much so that the local Aussies call it Vietnamatta.

'But even if he had a woman stashed in Cabramatta, what was he doing in the backblocks of Strathfield? If he'd been on his way home, the heart attack would have hit him somewhere on the Hume Highway, surely?'

'You think he might have died somewhere else and somebody moved him?' asked Lizzie. 'That would be pretty risky. What if the cops pulled them up; how would they explain a politician's body in the boot?'

'That makes me think it wasn't a married woman who didn't want publicity. I think it was somebody who couldn't afford a visit from the police.'

'Do you think Brabazon was mixed up in the Cabramatta rackets?'

'Maybe. He was very careful to make sure nobody knew where he was that night.'

'So all you have to do is find the Vietnamese restaurant Brabazon ate at,' said Lizzie.

'Nobody in Cabramatta is going to tell me. The Vietnamese make the bloody Mafia look talkative.'

'Who've you tried?' asked Lizzie.

'No one yet. I need a Vietnamese with an axe to grind.'

'Or an Aussie with a good nose,' said Lizzie. 'What about Laurie?'

Laurie Saunders was a journo who'd put together a documentary on the Vietnamese in Australia for ABC TV, and had picked up a Walkley award. He was free that night for a drink.

Laurie was straight out of *Countrywide* — blond and boyish, with jeans, a tweed jacket and elastic-sided boots. He was sporting a three-day growth which made him look sexy and would have made me look like one of the Beagle Boys.

'Christ, Syd, you must have hit the jackpot,' he said, surveying the Intercontinental's price list, the pin-striped clientele, the potted palms and the chamber orchestra.

'Expenses, mate.'

'Still driving the Valiant, though,' he said.

I bit. 'It's got more class than a bloody Holden station wagon.'

'I need it for the equipment,' he defended. 'And anyway, nobody ever made a living out of docos.'

I didn't need anyone else's hard luck stories. 'Tell me about the rackets in Cabramatta, Laurie.'

'The works,' he said. 'Some pretty tough customers baled out of Saigon at the last minute. Crims, pimps, people like that.'

'Our allies, you mean?'

'Yeah, you know, political refugees.'

After we'd stopped laughing he said: 'For starters, the Chinese

Triads are moving in from Hong Kong, and I hear they're recruiting ethnic Chinese for the narcotics business. Plus there's the usual stuff—protection for shopkeepers, teenage gangs with knives and aggro between gambling outfits. It's been kept very quiet; nobody's game to make a noise in case they get branded a racist.'

'So it's bad.'

'It's no worse than the Italian and Lebanese scams, but some of the Vietnamese solve arguments with knives or guns and that hits the news. It makes people nervous. And it's hard for the cops to get any leads because of the language problem and because the victims won't complain.'

'Because they're scared?'

'Partly. And they don't trust the cops any more than they trust their own hoods. Besides, they don't want to give the racists any ammunition. What's this for, by the way?'

'Can you keep your mouth shut?'

'Depends.'

'There might be a story in it.'

'I can keep my mouth shut if you'll give me first crack at the story but I won't wait forever.'

It was the best I could get, and I still needed Laurie, so I agreed to give him an exclusive. I'd worry about Lizzie later. 'Barbara Brabazon's got me looking into Jack Brabazon's death,' I said.

'But he was supposed to have had a heart attack.'

'Yeah, but he had a heart attack between Cabramatta and the North Shore, and he'd been eating Vietnamese food, and his family didn't know where he was.'

Laurie's eyebrows shot up. 'Brabazon was a professional Vietvet, wasn't he?'

'Yes. That means he must have been close to at least a few Vietnamese out there. I'd like to know who.'

'I'll ask around,' he said.

We had a couple more drinks that would have cost a Vietnamese waiter two hours' pay each, and talked about Brabazon. Laurie asked me what I'd thought of Deborah.

'Too buttoned up,' I said. 'I like my women more, you know... I can't stand those North Shore women who look as if they'd turn on their meters the minute you got them into the sack.'

'You're mad,' Laurie said. 'They're great. They're always married to some fat, boring bastard who works fourteen hours a day and lusts after the office girls. Those women go off like rockets when you rip their designer dresses off.'

'You've done this before,' I said.

'Bet your arse,' he said, smirking.

While he was feeling mellow I asked if he could find someone to do some snooping in Cabramatta, someone who blended in. 'I'll need someone who doesn't scare easily and who won't rat to his friends.'

'Ricky Tan,' he said.

'Who's he?'

'Ethnic Chinese, brought up in Vietnam. Wants to be an investigative journalist.'

'A noble aspiration,' I said, and Laurie snorted with laughter. 'But isn't that unusual for a Vietnamese?'

'His brother got roughed up over a gambling debt, I heard. I think he's got a few scores to settle. Plus he's on the make politically, and thinks there might be votes in protecting the little people.'

'Is he tough?'

'No, but he's smart, fast and very ambitious.'

Laurie said he'd put Ricky Tan in touch with me and we parted. 'Don't forget,' he said. 'You owe me.'

The following day I took Parramatta Road and the Hume Highway out to Cabramatta. I hadn't been there in years so it was a surprise. A pleasant one.

It might have looked like downtown Saigon, but it was a vast improvement on the dreary working-class suburbs full of depressed single mums that surrounded it. The street and shop signs were bilingual, as were the Vietnamese shopkeepers; wonderful smells wafted out of dozens of restaurants; Vietnamese delis displayed livers, trotters, gizzards; there were video shops stocking only Vietnamese movies; and fruit shops sold vegetables I'd never seen before.

I bought a couple of the last fifty cent croissants in Sydney, and stoked up on *bo nuong* in a big, ramshackle fast-food complex that resembled an open-air market with a roof, then drove back into town to Kensington.

I needed to know more about Jack Brabazon: you can't understand a death without a life.

I had interviewed Dr Greg Hazlehurst once for a newspaper feature on Agent Orange, and we'd hit it off. Greg taught history at the University of New South Wales, and was a Vietnam veteran. He was available for a chat after a three o'clock tutorial.

Greg had started life as an old-fashioned working-class patriot, had done well at Duntroon and finished up in Vietnam. In Phuoc Tuy he'd changed his mind about Australia's involvement and subsequently left the army, learned Vietnamese and French and found his way into academia.

'Brabazon was your typical politician in some ways,' Greg told me. 'An operator. Always on. But he did have a few beliefs. He did care about Vietnam; in fact, I'm almost sure he went back with a parliamentary delegation in '78 or '79.'

'He can't have been much of an operator if he got called up.'

'He didn't get called up, mate. He volunteered.'

'Why would someone like Brabazon volunteer?'

'Maybe he was trying to save the world from communism.'

'Personally? I thought the idea was to send the proletariat in while you finished your law degree at Sydney University.'

Greg laughed. 'It did occur to me that he might have been trying to get away from his mother.'

I could sympathise with that. 'Did it work?'

'Yeah. He had a good time when he wasn't getting shot at or shitting himself about stepping on a mine. He loved it.'

'Vietnam?'

'Nam. The war, the people. Fish sauce.'

'Fish sauce?'

'Fish sauce. The Vietnamese use it on everything. One snort of fish sauce and you're right back there. Very nostalgic.'

'So he had a good war?'

'He had a great war. He actually became human for the first time in his life. He even fell in love with a Vietnamese girl. It lasted nine months. Next thing I knew, he'd married Deborah White, got preselection and was away and running. The boy statesman.'

We talked about how the Vietnam War was back in the news again and how the breach between those who marched away and those who marched in the streets was healing at last. All the protagonists were turning forty and were mellowing a bit. The veterans had staged rallies in the run-up to the Bicentenary, and thousands had turned out; to cheer this time. A lot of people, myself included, had been quite moved by the sight.

My curiosity got the better of me. 'Explain one thing to me, Greg. What makes a bloke like you join the army?'

He stared off into his past for a while, then said: 'It ran in the family, I suppose. My grandfather got out of Gallipoli alive, and my father was at Tobruk and Shaggy Ridge. When I was a kid, I found an old trunk in the garage full of uniforms and medals and stuff. That was the start of it.'

I'd marched against the Vietnam war with the rest of them and prayed my number wouldn't come up. I wasn't sure which would be worse, the Vietcong or the warders at Long Bay.

Greg knew most of the influential Vietnamese in Cabramatta, so I asked him to do me a favour. We went back to his office and he rang the editor of a Vietnamese-language newspaper and quizzed him about where Jack Brabazon might have hung out in the area, and who his special friends might have been.

He got nowhere.

'Not knowing or not talking?' I asked.

'Scared, I think. Very interesting.'

Before I left he asked me to let him know if I found out anything suspicious about Brabazon's death.

'Is your interest personal or political?'

'The personal is the political,' he said and we laughed, remembering the sixties. 'Actually, a bit of both. I know he came on like Andrew Peacock sometimes, but when he was in Nam away from his mother, he was quite a likeable bastard. Very funny. And charming when it suited him. I suppose that's what got him into Deborah White's pants. How's she taking it, by the way?'

'I don't know,' I confessed. 'There's something weird there.

Brabazon's women fought over him when he was alive, I'd say, and I think some sort of battle is still going on, but they're not letting me in on it.'

Deborah Brabazon's reaction to her husband's death had been nagging me, so I made an appointment to see her again. She was unenthusiastic, but agreed, perhaps because it would look bad to hamper the investigation.

'The autopsy report said he'd been eating Vietnamese food,' I said, when I'd got myself comfortably settled on her English chintz couch with a cup of coffee.

She grew very still. 'He often does... did. He was an old Vietnam hand, you know.'

'You weren't invited?'

'I don't care for it,' she said, leaving me to figure out whether she meant the politics, the people or the cuisine.

'Did he have a favourite restaurant?'

'Not that I know of. Really, I don't know. That part of his life was... his own.'

'His mother wants to know where he spent his last hours, Mrs Brabazon. Aren't you curious?'

She turned and stared out the window so I couldn't see her face. 'It won't make any difference,' she said. 'It won't bring him back.'

I couldn't argue with that.

I got back to my office to find a message from Laurie Saunders. 'The Baria Restaurant in John Street, Cabramatta,' it said. 'Apparently he's been going there for years. And don't forget: this is my story.'

Ricky Tan turned up in my office that evening — thin, intense and dressed to kill in pleated baggy pants, winkle pickers and a James Dean haircut. Multiculturalism, indeed.

'Laurie says you want to be a newspaperman.'

'Yes, but so far my English is not good enough. I am still studying. Also cooking in a noodle shop, Mr Fish.'

'So you need the dough?'

'Dough?'

'Ancient Australian slang for money,' I explained.

'Ah,' he said and stored it away. 'And perhaps also what you call a pun, Mr Fish?'

Laurie was right: the kid was quick.

'What do you want me to do, Mr Fish?'

I kept thinking I'd seen Ricky Tan somewhere before, until I realised he reminded me of Charlie Chan's Number One Son, full of mad ideas and dangerous enthusiasms. I hoped I was wrong.

'I want you to photograph everyone who goes in and out of the Baria Restaurant,' I said. 'And don't get caught.'

'What are you looking for, Mr Fish?'

'I don't know exactly.'

'You don't know?' Ricky was polite; he didn't raise his voice or tell me I was mad.

'No, but I might recognise it when I see it,' I said, and he left mulling that over.

By lunchtime next day I'd received a set of photo proofs from Ricky Tan, so I asked Barbara Brabazon to get me in to see someone at police headquarters who knew about the Cabramatta milieu.

A couple of hours later I was in the office of a cleancut young undercover policeman who declined to identify himself. He took the photos away and returned with several names. I was particularly interested in a sleek prosperous looking type shown leaving the Baria with a woman and a teenage girl and entering a late-model Audi driven by a very tough looking chauffeur.

The man was in his forties, well fed and expensively dressed with dark glasses masking his expression. His wife was small and exquisite if a touch flashy, and the young girl took after her. The cop told me his name was Nguyen Van Thanh and that he owned the restaurant. I asked what else Thanh was into, but the cop refused to say. He'd been told to stay on the right side of me because of Barbara Brabazon's clout but he didn't like it. 'It's confidential,' he growled.

I drew my own conclusions. Even if restaurants are a cash business, it takes a lot of *cha gio* to buy a minder. It had to be drugs, vice, gambling, or all of the above.

The case was beginning to interest me. Brabazon's connection with the Baria could be perfectly innocent: Thanh might simply be a Vietnamese connection dating back seventeen years. But whatever Thanh had been in the old country, he was known to the

Australian organised crime bodies, so what was a Federal Opposition frontbencher doing dining regularly in a restaurant owned by a Vietnamese hood? Too many politicians had bitten the dust in New South Wales lately for consorting with criminals for Brabazon to have been unaware of the risks.

That afternoon I got a call from a social worker at Westmead Hospital. Mr Tan was in hospital, injured, and wanted to see me.

Ricky's head was bandaged, his eyes blackened, and his face covered in cuts turning dark yellow with Betadine.

'What the fuck happened to you?' I asked.

'I think someone did not like me taking photographs. A man grabbed me and smashed my camera.'

'And your face.'

'That will heal, Mr Fish, but the camera cost five hundred dollars.'

A realist. 'Don't get your Nikon in a knot, Ricky. We'll reimburse you. Who was the man?'

He said he thought it was Mr Thanh's driver. So he knew the owner's name.

'The cops are on to Thanh for something,' I said. 'And it looks to me like organised crime. What have you heard about him?'

'I have only heard whispers, Mr Fish. These men are very bad. People don't dare say their names.'

I persisted. 'What are they whispering?'

His eyes darted nervously round the room. 'Heroin,' he murmured. 'It's said he does business with the Hong Kong Chinese.'

I asked Ricky if he needed anything — grapes, an Agatha Christie novel, a copy of Strunk and White? He assured me his family would look after him. I told him to come and see me about his fee when he could walk. It occurred to me that he was taking his beating surprisingly well, but I put it down to bravado.

The bashing had confirmed my suspicion that we were dealing with a serious heavy, but what was his connection with Jack Brabazon?

The answer came three days later from an unexpected quarter — Barbara Brabazon.

The Brabazon maid appeared more confused than ever and when she ushered me into the living room, I understood why. It seemed to be full of people, Vietnamese people: a woman and a girl, to be exact, and Ricky Tan, who was so excited he was dancing — if it's possible to dance sitting down.

Barbara Brabazon sailed into the room and asked if I would like some tea. I declined.

'I expect you're wondering why Mr Tan is here?' she asked.

'I was rather,' I said, noticing that Ricky was avoiding my eye.

'Mr Tan has found my grand-daughter,' said the old lady, and my eyes flew to the girl, who was sitting stiffly on the couch, hands folded, eyes huge.

'That's your grand-daughter?'

'Yes, Nguyen Thi My. My, for short. And that's her mother, Dinh.'

As soon as we were introduced, I realised they were the woman and girl photographed with Thanh coming out of the Baria. Close up, I could tell the girl was Eurasian. I cursed myself for not noticing earlier, the price of ethnocentricity. Ricky Tan had obviously picked it up straight away.

I didn't believe for a moment Ricky Tan was acting alone, though; I thought I detected the fine hand of his mentor, Laurie Saunders. He certainly had his story now.

Mrs Brabazon excused us and led me away to her study. She told me Dinh was the girl Jack met while he was serving in Vietnam and My had been conceived then. He had looked for her when he returned in 1979 with a parliamentary delegation, and Dinh had put pressure on Jack to get her and his daughter into Australia. Dinh's brother, Nguyen Van Thanh came as part of the deal.

That would have suited Brabazon, I thought. Moving them into Turramurra with Deborah might have proven a bit tricky, and the brother-in-law could look after his little family for him. Unfortunately for Jack, the new brother-in-law had quickly found his level in his new country — rock bottom. I decided Jack must have known but preferred the risks involved with Thanh to fronting the Brabazon women with the story.

I doubted that Dinh had filled Barbara Brabazon in on all her brother's business activities, and I had no intention of ruining the moment for the old woman. Anyway, if Saunders were on the story, it wouldn't stay secret for long.

'Have you found out what happened the night Jack died?' I asked.

'Dinh said Jack had the heart attack at her house and died instantly. She wanted to call the police but her brother wouldn't let her. He drove Jack's car to Strathfield and left it there.'

She was teetering on the edge of some dangerous silences, but I couldn't blame her. This new relationship was going to be complicated enough without asking Dinh if she'd helped move Jack's body. Or if Jack might have been saved if they'd called a doctor. Those sorts of questions don't go away, though.

'Dinh and My will be coming to live with me, now,' she said. She looked years younger: Jack might be gone, but she had some part of him.

Because it had turned out so well, she gave me a small bonus. I didn't ask how much Ricky Tan had creamed off the top. It would have been ungracious, and besides, without Ricky's sharp eyes and entrepreneurial flair, the long-lost grand-daughter might have lived out her days above a restaurant in Cabramatta. Or at least until her uncle had decided to cash her in.

Saunders's treachery was the only loose end in the case. This wasn't the first time he'd shafted me, either. I stewed about it all the way home; then I called Lizzie and gave her an exclusive on the Brabazon case.

WASTED LIVES

'Don't look for me, I'm not coming back. Sean.' said the note, which was written on paper torn from a school exercise book.

The man who handed it to me seemed beaten, as if his job ate him up or his life had taken a wrong turning too far back. A big fair man going to fat, Dean Somers had starburst veins on the cheeks and pouches under the eyes.

'He's our only child,' he said, handing me a photograph.

'Is he old enough to leave home?' I asked, surveying the skinny, sandy-haired teenager with flat, secretive eyes.

'Is anyone ever old enough to leave home?' he asked, and I revised my opinion upwards slightly. Seeing my grin, he said: 'Technically, yes. He's sixteen. But he's a very young sixteen.'

'How is he financing this?'

'He's got credit cards.'

'So he could last quite a while on his own. Unless you turn off the tap...'

'We don't want to do that,' he said quickly. 'If he comes back, we want it to be voluntary. I'm not hiring you to kidnap him off the streets; I want you to find him and talk to him. See if he's OK.'

'How's his mother taking this?'

A look that could have been indigestion but was more likely pain crossed his face. 'Hard. Sharon is... the nervous type. She's all for dragging Sean home by the hair. She's worried about what the neighbours will say.'

As they lived in St Ives, I doubted the neighbours would be in a position to judge. A very expensive North Shore suburb full of desperadoes living beyond their means in huge mansions and beating their wives to alleviate the tensions of social climbing, St Ives reputedly suffers the highest rate of family breakdown in Sydney.

'Did you see this coming?' I asked. 'Did he seem that unhappy?'

'How would I know?' he said, truculent. 'I work eighteen hours a day. I hardly ever see the kid and when I do he grunts and scuttles away. I thought that was normal.'

'How does he get on with his mother?'

'Sharon is a perfectionist. Everything has to be just so. I suppose she was on his back a lot, but you'd think he'd be used to it by now.' He paused: 'I am.'

I thought I detected a twinge of regret that he wasn't the one who'd got away. The big guy seemed pretty harmless and likeable and he probably gave in to Sharon to keep the peace. Maybe the kid felt outnumbered.

Wanting to take a look at Sean's belongings, I followed Somers' navy blue BMW out to St Ives. The house was vintage North Shore — a white two-storey mansion with green shutters, a driveway, double garage, manicured gardens and the inevitable swimming pool and barbecue pit. All it needed was a cardboard cutout nuclear family and a shaggy dog to make the cover of *Vogue Living*.

Sharon, who flew to the window at the first crunch of gravel, turned out to be a thin, avid bottle blond with a leathery tan and aerobics legs. She was the kind of woman whose insecurities drove her too far in every direction: the hairdo was too done, the diamonds too big for the daytime, the makeup too obvious and the manner too intense.

At her insistence, we got the full afternoon tea with silver tea service, Wedgwood china, Sara Lee chocolate cake and cake forks. The last time I'd seen a cake fork was in the parlour of a Sisters of Mercy convent in 1960.

As far as Sharon was concerned, everything between herself and her son was hunky dory. He was a wonderful boy who'd never given her any trouble and she was astonished and shocked at his defection.

Realising I wasn't going to get any change out of Sean's mother, I smiled and forked up chocolate cake and tried to pick up the truth from the ether.

The house reeked of obsession. It was frighteningly clean and no child or animal would have dared pollute its perfection. Sharon had learned enough not to leave plastic sheets on the furniture but it felt as if she had. In the downstairs toilet, tiny fruit-shaped soaps stood to attention on the washbasin, and I hardly dared sully the pristine guest towels. It felt like a doll's house with a giant Sharon looming above watching every move.

Sean's room was unnaturally tidy for a teenager's lair. If the kid had a life, he didn't carry it on in this house. Besides posters featuring Bon Jovi and Batman and some schoolbooks — nothing. There had to be more. And there was, a computer desk minus computer.

'He took his computer?' I asked Sharon.

'Yes. He loved that thing.'

'What was it?'

'An Amiga.'

'What did he use it for, schoolwork?'

'Playing those stupid games, I suppose. He was always buying new programs for it, I know that.'

'Was he interested in art?'

'Not that I know of. Why?'

'I'm pretty sure Amigas are designed for computer graphics,' I said. 'Did he ever show you any of his stuff?'

Choosing to be offended rather than admit she didn't know anything about Sean's hobbies, she snapped: 'I'm not one of those mothers who goes poking around in her child's things. I give him his privacy.'

She flounced off, leaving me free to poke around. Between the bed and the wall I found a chrome Volkswagen logo. It didn't seem to fit the kid, somehow; this family would rather hock their souls than drive a cheap car. Unless Sean got his kicks joyriding.

I followed Sharon Somers down the stairs and joined the couple in the living room. 'What do you think?' asked the boy's father.

'Is Sean interested in cars?'

They looked at each other in genuine surprise.

'No,' said Dean. 'He can drive the BMW and Sharon's Accord, of course, but he's not a petrolhead. Why?'

I showed them the VW logo. They were mystified, but said I could take it with me. I asked if it would be OK for me to talk to the kid's teachers and friends; some people didn't like publicising their family affairs in show and tell.

'Oh, I don't...' began his mother, but Dean interrupted. 'You might as well talk to the school. He wasn't happy there anyway, and I'm not sending him back when he comes home.'

A rush of anger reddened Sharon's thin cheeks and receded, leaving her pale and pinch lipped. I knew then the 'right' school was very important to her, and there would be repercussions. As soon as Dean started making the phone calls to get me in to see Sean's form master, she stalked out the room.

'What about his friends?' I asked before I set out on the drive to the city.

'I don't know. He went to Turramurra High till he was fourteen, and he used to run around with some kid there, but I haven't seen him around for a year or more and I can't even remember his name. I've never seen Sean with any of the boys from Harbourside; at least he's never asked anyone here.'

With Dean Somers' unhappy pudgy face in my rear vision mirror, I left them to their domestic and headed back along the Pacific Highway.

I'd been curious about Harbourside since I'd worked with an Arts editor who'd told me he had 'a perfect Harbourside accent.'

The school itself squatted jealously on one of Sydney's prime harbour frontages and had the usual sprinkling of dark ivy-clad brick and lots of ugly new sixties and seventies extensions, testament to the profitability of privelege. A frosty middle-aged woman, probably the mother of an ex-pupil, asked me to wait while she called Sean Somers' form master from a class, and kept her eye on me in case I pinched any of the school memorabilia or sporting trophies.

Robert Standish turned out to be mid-thirties, balding, weedy and tweedy in a Mr Chips sort of way, and unless I miss my guess, a very discreet homosexual. Too old to flaunt, too young for radical celibacy. I wondered briefly what it would be like teaching in the sort of school where the pupils would automatically regard teachers as social failures.

Standish didn't seem to have any obvious inferiority complex, however, and dealt efficiently with my inquiries. What he told me convinced me that Sean was part of the sludge that settled to the bottom of any school, not particularly good at anything, not popular and scarcely remembered by classmates in later life unless they joined a band and died of drug abuse or went into law and got caught embezzling widows' trust funds.

'Was he happy here?' I asked.

'Not really. He was very young for his age, immature. He didn't actually cause any trouble but there was something resistant about him. He didn't want to be here.'

'Where did he want to be?'

'At some state high school, probably. He always gave me the impression he regarded this place as a jail.'

He liked this metaphor, and expanded on it. 'Come to think of it, he acted like a model prisoner planning a break out. Keeping a low profile, making no waves. A born passive resister. At a big state high he would have been left alone to get on with what he wanted to do.'

'Which was what?'

'I don't know, but any kid who works that hard at being invisible has to have some sort of secret life.'

As I recalled, secret lives were not unknown at Harbourside: a couple of years before the cops had cracked a ring of seniors forging IDs so they could drink at trendy pubs and pick up girls.

I thanked him and asked if I could talk to any of the boy's special friends, but he didn't have any, it seemed. Instead I was steered to the form captain, a big, brawny, well-mannered and well-spoken youth, who may even have possessed the perfect Harbourside accent. Julian Braithwaite had impeccable credentials for leadership — no sense of humour, total self-confidence and a complete lack of imagination.

'Somers didn't fit in here,' he told me, probably sounding just like his father.

'Why?'

'He wasn't bright academically and he wasn't interested in rowing. He just didn't participate.'

'Maybe it wasn't his fault.'

He bridled. 'There are all sorts of programs here for average students; you don't have to be a genius. He never did any of them. He didn't try.'

'But he didn't have a single friend,' I said. 'Isn't that a bit unusual, even for a nerd?'

He blushed. My needling had finally got under his guard. 'You can't blame the school for the fact that Sean Somers was a loser. He just wasn't one of us. If you want to blame anybody, take a look at his mother.'

I pounced. 'What about his mother?'

But he knew he'd gone too far: it was OK to be a snob but you had to choose your audience these days. 'I think I should get back,' he said, shaking my hand with the synthetic warmth of an insurance salesman or a QC seeking preselection.

I watched him stride back to his classroom, a complete stranger to self-doubt, absolutely certain of his place in the universe, and wondered if these kids ingested pomposity with their mother's milk or learned it at school. If Julian Braithwaite had a secret life, it would centre on *Playboy* magazine.

As I drove across the Bridge I pondered the stupidity of parents who hocked their souls to have their children taught to look down on them. I also thought about the sorts of homes and schools where kids had to explode to be noticed. That led on to some reminiscences about my home life and relationship with my parents, and I decided I didn't really have the right to judge.

But where the hell was he?

At my office was a message from Sean's teacher: he'd asked around, and some of the kids had apparently seen Sean occasionally at Pymble station with a youth wearing a Turramurra High uniform. Maybe he had a friend after all.

So I rang the headmaster of Turramurra High, explained the situation and asked if any of Sean Somers' old teachers were still around. With so many teachers leaving the system to go into real estate or grow herbs in the Blue Mountains, I wasn't optimistic.

He said it was a big school and he'd have to check the boy's file and get back to me.

Instead, a woman called Cathy Cartwright called. She'd had the boy in her general studies class for a year before he left for Harbourside.

'What's this all about?' she asked.

'The kids's done a bunk and the parents want him back.'

'I'm not surprised. About the leaving, I mean. A very alienated little person, that one. Can we talk about this face to face?'

I agreed. Her voice had conjured up a tall athletic woman with a honey-blond pony tail and good teeth. The reality, when I met her for a drink in the beer garden at The Oaks, was a small, dark woman of about thirty with bouncy curls, navy blue eyes and a few freckles strategically placed for maximum cuteness.

We shook hands and sussed each other out. She must have decided I was a human being because she warmed up considerably and quizzed me closely about my job. Maybe she was thinking about a career change. All this was giving me a warm glow but wasn't helping me find Sean Somers, so I steered her back to the kid.

She told me he was average. 'At least that's the way he wanted to look. Sean went out of his way to act like wallpaper. Mind you, it's not that hard in a big school. They can be very overpowering, anonymous places. A lot of kids are stunned for a while, but most of them come to life eventually. Sean didn't.'

'What was his problem?'

'I don't know. I couldn't get him to talk, but I think he must have had something else going, outside school. He was pathologically secret.'

'Could he have been stealing cars?'

Her eyebrows flew up: 'What makes you think that?'

'Something I found in his room.'

She pondered. 'I don't think so. It feels wrong somehow, but I can't explain why.'

'What about his friends?'

'Friend,' she said. 'He only had one. God, doesn't that sound awful, most kids have dozens, but poor old Sean only had Brian.'

'Brian?'

'Brian the dork. Pimples, clammy hands, no discernible talents, single mum. That Brian.'
'Other name?'
'Something alliterative.'
'Brown, Boru?'

She laughed and shook her head. I went and charmed the bar attendant out of the pub's phone book and we ran through the Bs. We hit the jackpot at Buckley. Seeing the number of Buckleys, she said she'd get the mother's name tomorrow and call me.

I thanked her and asked if she'd like to have dinner some time and she said yes, it would be a nice change. No doubt I'd find out from what, later. Fairly satisfied with the progress of my private life, if not with my case, I went home and ate Mexican takeout, looked at the TV program and read a book. Times are bad when I'm driven to a book, but mismanagement and greed had turned television into the sort of artistic wasteland where *Beach Blanket Bingo* rated three stars.

At what was probably her morning tea break, Cathy Cartwright called me next day and gave me Brian Buckley's address. She said he seemed to have left the school.

The Buckleys lived in a small, rundown bungalow in the least salubrious part of Pymble. The door was opened by an old woman, and I hazarded a guess that it was her house, and her daughter and grandson had come home to roost when the marriage broke down. They appeared to be living on two pensions.

The house looked as if time had stood still since VE Day, and the furniture was the sort of wartime retro that fashionable gays kill for. Rita Buckley was fortyish and running to fat, but still fighting the grey in her hair with a rather violent shade of red. Her smile turned south when I told her I wanted to talk to her son about Sean Somers.

'He's not home,' she said angrily.
'Where can I get him?'
'He's gone to Queensland to stay with his father.'
'How long will he be gone?' I asked.

The woman and her mother exchanged a look I couldn't read: 'At least three months.'

'Maybe you can help me,' I said, desperate. 'Sean Somers has run away from home and I'm trying to locate him. Is it possible he's with your boy?'

Her laughter was shrill: 'No, absolutely not.'

'I've heard Brian is Sean's best friend...' I began.

The woman cut me off: 'Sean Somers is no friend to Brian. He's a bad influence. It's all his fault...'

She started to cry, and her mother moved to comfort her, giving me a baleful glance over the heaving shoulders.

'You'd better leave, young man. You've upset Rita enough as it is. We don't like Sean Somers in this house. If he's gone, it's good riddance to bad rubbish as far as we're concerned.'

I left. It looked to me as if Brian Buckley's family had shipped him out to get him away from Sean. Perhaps this had tipped Sean over the edge.

It felt like a dead end, so I called Lizzie and asked if she wanted lunch. We met at the Malaya and scalded our mouths with chicken laksa and extinguished the flames with too much white wine, and I asked Lizzie what sort of secret life a sixteen-year-old boofhead might be conducting.

'Clues?'

I didn't have the note with me but I recited it from memory.

'Typed or handwritten?' Catching my expression, she said: 'It's always important in Agatha Christies.'

I suspected Lizzie of not taking this seriously, but I played along. 'Printed.'

'What sort of notepaper?'

I sighed. 'A scrap of school exercise book with some sort of list on the back.'

'List?'

'Colours, I guess. The kid seemed to have been interested in art, but nobody's seen any of his...'

'Oeuvre?'

'...pictures. He's got an Amiga and lots of heavy software according to his parents. He took the PC with him.'

'What were the colours?' interrupted Lizzie, and I could hear an idea stirring in her voice.

'I think it said something like 2 black, 2 white, 2 sky blue, 2 military blues, 2 pinks.'

'Ah. Other clues?'

'Only a chrome VW logo. Maybe he steals VWs.'

'Jackpot!' crowed Lizzie. 'Mate, you're talking to the right lady. You've got a writer on your hands.'

'A writer?'

'A graffitist! A spraypainter! A bomber!'

'Are you sure?'

'VW stands for Vandals Wanted. You can't be more explicit that that.'

'How the hell did you know that? No, let me guess, you did a story on graffiti.'

'Yes. It was fascinating. The list you've got is called a shopping list. A kid who designs a tag...'

'What's a tag?'

'The initials you see all over walls and trains—they can be some kid's name or a gang signature.'

'Such as?'

'Such as OSB for One Step Beyond, or CC for Crime City, or RSL for Resist Sydney's Laws. As I was saying, a kid who comes up with a good tag can sell the design, along with a colour chart. Whoever buys it has to stick to the design and steal the spraypaints. They'd rather be caught dead than buying their supplies.'

'Did the kids tell you this?'

'No, I interviewed Tony Frost down at the transport police.'

'Maybe Sean is mixed up with a gang,' I said.

'It depends on whether he's got a taste for danger or not. Kids are always getting their heads knocked off hanging out carriage doors bombing the sides of trains. And the cops say gang members mug passengers and break into hardware stores and paint warehouses. And there was that girl some of them were supposed to have kidnapped in Sutherland and murdered, remember?'

I wasn't sure yet that Sean was a bomber, but it seemed likely that he was a designer. He certainly had all the gear, even a colour printer.

'Why don't you go and see Tony Frost,' suggested Lizzie. 'He loves to talk about his work.'

I found the transport police in Mary Street near Central Station in an area rapidly redeveloping into glass and brick canyons. Their office, with its scarred desks, railway issue lockers and mug shots of graffitists on the walls, was located in a dingy sixties lowrise with an air of impermanence.

Sergeant Frost was a tough old railway cop who knew his quarry as well as a ferret knows a rabbit and loved the chase. He was going to paunch but looked strong. I asked if he'd heard of Sean Somers and he said no, but when I showed him the kid's photo, he roared laughing.

'That's Sad Sack,' he said. 'I've been chasing him for two years. His tag's all over the Hornsby line—SS. I only ever caught sight of him once, but I never forget a face. Recognise the pimples, too. Where is the bugger?'

'Good question,' I said. 'What about Brian Buckley; do you know him?'

'I certainly do. He's taking a little rest cure at Cobham juvenile detention centre right this minute, courtesy of the transport police.'

'It fits,' I said. 'His mother blames Sean Somers for leading him astray.'

'Quite probable,' said Frost. 'Buckley's a born follower. What did you say you wanted with Sad Sack?'

'He's baled out of home and his folks have hired me to get him back.'

'Must have plenty of money,' said Frost, fishing.

'St Ives, Somers Building Supplies, Harbourside School.'

'Why did they let the little punk run around wasting trains?' he asked.

'They didn't know. I haven't told them yet. His mother's very highly strung; she'll climb the wall.'

'Let's find him,' said the cop. 'We've got a picture and a name. Plenty of these kids owe me favours. I'll call some in.'

After some urging and a check with his superiors, Frost agreed to take me out on the beat to show Sean's photo around. While he was on the phone two young men came in wearing gelled hair, mittens, jeans, expensive leather jackets, cowboy boots and designer sneers.

'Undercover cops,' volunteered Frost and introduced us.

I asked one of them if that was a gang uniform.

'Nah. They wear any old shit but they like nice gear,' said Smiley. 'So you'd better watch out if you've got a good leather jacket. If it's their size, they'll hold a knife on you and rip it off your back. And if you put up a fight they'll chuck you off the train.'

'Yeah,' said the other. 'They're kind of like, you know, socialists.' They laughed.

While they regaled me with graffiti folk lore, Frost showed me a folder full of colour photos of wasted trains and daubed walls. My eye lingered for a moment on a railway bridge sporting the slogan WASTED LIVES. And on a polaroid of a train with an entire panel sprayed with the logo SS in black, red and white.

On Friday nights every bored juvenile in Sydney is out, most of them in George Street hanging around the cinema complexes: we headed there. After a stop at the police's branch office on Central Station, we took the train to Town Hall.

In George Street the din was tremendous—hoons in V8s screaming tyres and thundering rap music from car radios, crowds of hormone-driven teenagers horsing around, families with whingeing kids streaming in and out of the theatres, buskers murdering a variety of musical instruments, and people clumped around a pavement artist who was reproducing a portion of the Sistine Chapel in lurid chalk.

Oblivious, Frost took up a strategic position outside Hoyts. It was hilarious: groups of kids would bop towards us, spot Frost, do a doubletake and attempt to flee. A few made it; he pounced on the rest with the relentless efficiency of a cane toad hunting mice.

An elaborate ritual ensued. They'd eyeball each other suspiciously, Frost would smile like a friendly wolf, pleasantries would be exchanged, absent friends asked after (showing he had every kid's dossier in his head), and then Sad Sack's name would casually come up. When they denied all knowledge, I'd flash Sean's photo.

Finally a rat-faced underfed kid with a flat-top you could land a helicopter on said he'd seen him yesterday on Broadway, near Central.

'Where is he now?' I asked.

'Dunno,' said the kid.

I was getting bored. Frost eventually noticed and asked if I'd like to see some action on the trains. Anything to get away, I said. He suggested a coffee followed by a trip on the last train to Cronulla.

'That'll wake you up,' he said, and I didn't like the way he smiled.

The last train to Cronulla was full of drunken youths who hadn't scored and were not happy about it. A few couples huddled together trying not to attract attention. Everybody else in the southern suburbs was at home with the deadbolts drawn.

Most of the kids steered clear of us: we were oldies, yes, but we were also bigger than most of them and didn't look like sissies. When a couple of shoving matches broke out, Frost's concentration sharpened, but he sat tight. Most people got off at Sutherland, leaving the train with a curiously unprotected feeling. Frost sat staring ahead but I could feel the energy beside me and knew he had the whole carriage monitored.

Apart from two scruffy looking types acting a lot drunker than they probably were, there were only ourselves and a teenage couple and a dozing middle-aged businessman with a face like a deflated football, who'd stayed at the pub too long.

Suddenly the connecting door crashed open and three teenagers erupted into the carriage. Deciding the rest of us were too big or too poor, they advanced on the suit, surrounded him, jostled him awake and demanded his money. When he took too long to respond, one of the youths started shouting and menacing him.

This excited his mates, who pulled the dazed drunk to his feet and pushed him back and forward between them. Adrenalin pumping, I looked at Frost for direction. He shook his head and put a large restraining paw on my arm. Then I realised why. The two drunk teenagers leapt to their feet and charged the bully boys, one flashing his ID and telling them they were under arrest.

Naturally they took off like rockets, the cops on their heels. As the numbers were against the goodies, Frost gave me the nod. When one of the would-be muggers raced past, I tripped him and he fell into Frost's arms. The policeman quickly wrenched his arms behind his back and handcuffed him.

'Nice going,' I said.

Meanwhile the undercover men had pinned down the other two.

Cronulla Police Station was a quick forced march from the station. I went along; there wasn't anywhere else to go in Cronulla at 2 a.m. on a Saturday morning. Not if you were my age, anyway.

The kids were duly processed while I dozed in the depressing waiting room with only posters of Australia's most wanted criminals and warnings about drugs and firearms for distraction. Eventually Frost and his raiders appeared.

'Got something for you,' said Frost, flicking me a piece of paper. It was a cheap business card with a highly stylised SSC logo in one corner and a phone number in the centre.

'What is it?'

'Sad Sack Consultants,' answered Frost. 'Your little friend has set up his own business.'

'Doing what?'

'We'll find out tomorrow, won't we?' the policeman said mysteriously.

Reliving their night's triumphs endlessly, the undercover cops drove us back to the city. When I finally crawled into bed I had jumbled dreams about trains and tunnels, which would probably have intrigued Freud but left me exhausted.

'Couldn't the kid you arrested tell you about the card?' I asked Frost the following afternoon, drinking evil instant coffee out of a borrowed mug in his office at Central.

'Says not. Got it at a meeting.'

'A meeting!'

'Yeah, they're very organised, this lot. Have little meetings to swap intelligence. Tell each other which hardware stores to crack. Stuff like that. Anyway, Terry has agreed to help us out.'

Terry, when he was led into the interview room, was a shadow of his former cocky self. Wearing a threadbare denim jacket, dirty jeans, a Def Leppard tee shirt and motorcycle boots, he was wiry and stunted, with the wary look that comes from generations of experience of police power. By the time he was thirty, he'd have spent half his life in institutions and would be losing his teeth.

'You know what you're supposed to do, Terry,' said Frost.

'Yair.'

'Yair what?'

'Yair, Sergeant.'

Watching Frost at work it was clear he had no personal animosity towards his prey; in fact they seemed to respond well to his mix of macho force and rough kindness. I had a suspicion he'd been a lot like them at their age.

He sat Terry down, switched the phone to conference mode, dialled the number, put the handset into the kid's hand, and sat back for some theatre. The phone rang for a long time before a businesslike voice said: 'Yes?'

'Vis SSC?' inquired Terry.

'Yes.'

'Look, mate. Some of us heard you got somefink...'

'What do you call yourselves?' asked the voice.

'JFA,' said Terry. 'We're lookin for some place to bust, get cans, y'know...'

'That's your problem,' interrupted the voice. 'If you want a tag designed, I'll do that.'

'Izzat right, mate? Whaddya charge for a tag?'

'Fifty bucks.'

'Jeez! That's a lotta bread for a tag! We could do it for nuffink.'

'Take it or leave it,' came the answer. 'It's expensive because it's computer designed.' It was him all right. 'If you want to see an example of our work, check out the 5.50 from Hornsby tomorrow morning.' He hung up.

'You did good, Terry,' said Frost. 'I'll remember that.'

'Fifty bucks for a fuckin tag! He's mad!'

As he was being led out to return to Minda detention centre, I called out: 'What does JFA stand for, Terry?'

'Just Fuckin Around,' he called over his shoulder. 'We're famous, mate.'

'Are they?' I asked Frost.

He rolled his eyes heavenward and said: 'In certain circles, perhaps. Let's pull Somers in.'

An inquiry of Telecom revealed that the phone was located in a room in one of the old warehouses on Broadway. The decrepit building was a hotbed of failed capitalism, a warren of small, struggling businesses. Bent old Jewish jewellers co-existed peacefully with naturopaths, surgical appliance shops, a fortune teller, an outsize shoe shop and finally, SSC.

Despite its colourful sign SSC was empty. Frost was disappointed but undaunted. 'Might just check out the depot tonight,' he said. 'Want to come along and see your friend's handiwork?'

What could I do? By this time I was completely sucked in; besides, I knew where Sean operated from and could pull him in any time.

Freed for a time from the treadmill of a transport cop's life, I went back to my office, checked the mail, groaned over the phone bill and called Lizzie.

'I think we've found him. He's running a bloody graffiti design consulting company.'

'I think it's wonderful,' said Lizzie. 'We need entrepreneurial spirit in this country. Maybe he could get a grant from the federal government and export his designs to New York.'

'You're not taking this seriously,' I complained.

'Don't be so bloody moralistic. What you should be doing is figuring out a way of using his talents legally so he doesn't end up at bloody Bidura or some other hellhole hanging by his shoelaces.'

'What do I tell his parents?' I protested. 'To leave him alone because bombing trains fulfills some spiritual and artistic need? Give me a break.'

'Don't be so wet. Find him and put the options. Persuasively. Then talk to his parents and cut a deal. They'll probably do anything rather than risk a jailbird in the family. He needs to get away from that jock school and into an art college. The kid could probably make a fortune designing record covers or tee shirts.'

Save me from social workers, I thought, hanging up with a flea lodged firmly in my ear.

I thought of calling the Somers with a progress report, but decided I couldn't face Dean's hangdoggery or Sharon's barely controlled hysteria until I had talked to Sean. But Sharon, puffing furiously on a cigarette and pacing the parquet in St Ives, wanted her money's worth and rang me for a progress report. I answered reluctantly, prejudices securely in place, full of *Psychology Today* blame.

She interrogated me, found out I knew where Sean could be contacted, and asked me why I hadn't informed her. I said I was concerned about the boy and hadn't made up my mind how to approach him.

'You think that's your decision, do you, Mr Fish? Is that how you usually operate? Do you usually withhold information from your clients?'

I said it was complicated, that the boy was mixed up in something dodgy...

'Not drugs!' she interrupted, and the panic in her voice made me realise I'd have to tell her. 'No, he's in with some graffiti gangs, you know, spraypainting trains. He's gone into business for himself, designing graffiti.'

I'd expected horror and outrage—nobody like to hear their son is a vandal—but she was relieved. 'God, is that all. We can fix that...'

'I don't think it's that easy, Mrs Somers. That's a very unhappy, alienated kid you've got there...'

'I think you've misunderstood me,' she said. 'Of course the graffiti is a problem. Sean is a problem. I know that. But if you were standing in my shoes you'd realise what a relief it is.'

'Tell me, Mrs Somers, why is it a relief to you that your kid is a vandal who defaces public property for a living?'

My heavy sarcasm went over her head like an MX: she was thinking something over. 'All right, I'll tell you. You seem to have Sean's interests at heart, and maybe you'll be able to deal with him better if you know what's behind all this. Mr Fish, do you know much about the Sydney... milieu?'

'You mean the crims?'

'Yes, the crims.'

'Some. I've lived in Sydney long enough to know the score. And I read the *Sun Herald* and Bob Bottom.'

'So you would have heard of Noddy Wilson.'

I had. Noddy Wilson had been a vicious hood with a face like an axe blade and a mouth like the slot in a moneybox. He had the moral discrimination of a freshwater crocodile. As a toddler he would have tortured the Tooth Fairy and mugged Father Christmas. He'd been a household name in the forties and fifties, when Sydney's gangs held shoot-outs in nightclubs and in the streets of Elizabeth Bay. Word was he had left a fortune.

I stalled: I was being led, but I wasn't sure where.

'My maiden name was Wilson, Mr Fish. I am Noddy Wilson's daughter.'

It was a KO. I bounced once and lay still.

'Does Sean know that?'

'Of course not. I wouldn't wish that on any child. Do you remember what happened to Noddy Wilson?'

I didn't.

Sharon was relentless. 'He died in jail. Somebody stabbed him to death in the showers.'

The silence grew between us. She took pity on me and broke it: 'I was sixteen.'

'Sean's age.'

'Sean's age. Now I know what you think of me, Mr Fish...'

Guilty as hell, I tried to interrupt but she wasn't listening.

'Something has gone very wrong with my son and I'm prepared to admit that some of it is my fault. But blaming myself or my father or fate doesn't help, I've learned that through bitter experience. I want a chance to make it right. What's important is where we go from here.'

'So if I bring him home, you'll listen to what he says?'

'Yes. And I'll give him whatever he wants.'

'What if he wants out?'

She paused. That was the ultimate test: loving and letting go. 'We'll cross that bridge when we come to it.'

The night was cold and moonlit which was bad news for the bombers and good news for us. Dressed in black like a bunch of commandos, we staked out the depot as soon as it got dark, me fortified with a flask of rum, the others with coffee. I think.

The raiding party arrived at about midnight, three of them. They knew the guard's modus operandi well enough to wait for his tea break, and came in over the fence, all togged out in black and carting their supplies in army surplus kitbags. We'd all seen too many Steve McQueen movies.

My team went on red alert, fanning out quietly behind them, with orders not to pounce till they were red handed. I stayed where I was, well back, crouched behind a pile of disused sleepers. Then a movement caught my eye, another writer coming over the fence. He didn't join the others, but melted into the shadows, between me and the police.

While the cops were closing in on the bombers, I circled closer to the newcomer. As soon as the spraypainters began their urban beautification project, the police charged and all hell broke loose. Screaming warnings to each other, the bombers scattered, with howling cops in hot pursuit.

The melee drew my prey into the open, and when he stood up to get a better look at the action, I jumped him. With my considerable weight advantage, it wasn't hard to deck him, pinion his wrists and haul him to his feet.

It was a thin, fair youth in dark clothing and running shoes: 'Sad Sack, I presume,' I said.

The kid's eyes widened. When he got over the shock of being recognised by a stranger he thought was a cop, he said half-heartedly: 'Let me go, you bastard. I haven't done anything.'

'I'm not a cop,' I said. 'I'm working for your parents. They want you back.'

He was stunned for a moment, then regained his composure: 'They're dickheads...'

'That's beside the point,' I interrupted. 'Right now you have to get out of here before you get done for trespass.'

He stared at me. 'You're letting me go?'

'For now. I'll drop by your office tomorrow morning at nine to pick you up. You're going home.'

That floored him. Not only did I know him, I knew all about his little business venture as well.

'What if I refuse?'

'Look, Sean. The cops know your phone number and they've been to your office. They know what you do for a living. They can put you away for three months. With Brian.'

His face went stubborn, so I sweetened it: 'There is an alternative. I think you'll be allowed to go to art school.'

We were interrupted by loud voices as the police returned dragging a couple of protesting prisoners. When I turned to look, Sean took off, scaled the fence and disappeared.

It was late but it was important, so I rang the Somers household, said I thought I'd convinced Sean to come home and spent ten minutes talking Sharon out of driving into town to pick up her son in the morning.

SSC HQ was empty when I dragged in next day. Its managing director had bolted. The office door was ajar, so I went in. Sean had abandoned a desk, a filing cabinet and a failing dracaena, but his computer and printer were gone. Colour copies of his designs still festooned the walls: he was good.

Driving north to break the bad news, I pondered the mysteries of genes and heredity. No one seemed to know where the boy got his artistic talents, but it was pretty obvious where his ruthlessness had come from. He was going to need it, alone in the city, but I had no doubt he'd survive. In fact, I'd lay odds we'd all be hearing much more about Sean Somers before too long. One way or another.

For the moment, though, I was more worried about the immediate future, and what I was going to do with the note I'd found blue-tacked to SSC's wall. It read: 'Tell her I know.'

At the risk of a $40 on-the-spot fine, I eventually crumpled it into a ball and chucked it out the window somewhere on the Pacific Highway.

THE BUM'S RUSH

After two bottles of Hunter red, I was dreaming that a pile driver was pounding me into a hole in the foundations of a new Japanese hotel. Then I woke up and discovered that the pounding was coming from my front door. It was 3 a.m.

I dragged myself out of bed and shouted: 'I'm coming, for Christ's sake!' but it came out as a croak. When I saw who it was I felt even worse.

'Let me in, will ya, mate,' said the filthy wino at my door. It was Les. Les had been a mate of my father's since long before I was born. He'd always been around our house, luring my father to the pub and driving my mother mad.

Over the years the grog had shrunk Les from a beefy second rower for Easts to a wizened husk. I hadn't seen him since my father's funeral, and he'd gone downhill badly since then. He'd always been a drunk but now he was a wino, living rough.

His hands shook, his eyes looked boiled, and his clothes were stiff with dirt. While I was eyeing him off and trying to come up with a previous engagement, he was mumbling and doing a little dance and looking down the hall as if he expected a herd of spiders or a Martian raiding party.

Les had been good to me when I was a kid, slinging me a few bob when he had a win on the nags or the dogs, and he looked as if he might cark on my doorstep, so I let him in. I reeled back as he pushed past me—he stank like a bad pub on a Saturday morning.

'Got anything to drink,' he said, collapsing into a chair.

'Sorry,' I said, 'I'm all out of metho.'

When he started to moan I caved in and got him a beer. He drank it like a man who'd just outrun the DTs.

Slightly revived, he said: 'Can I stay here for a coupla days, Syd?'

'They chuck you out of Matthew Talbot at last?' I asked.

'It's serious, bugger you. There's some people after me.'

'Green people?' I asked.

'Dead set,' he moaned. 'Someone's tryin ta kill me. Garnet was sleeping in my bed last night and some bastard tried to set him alight. Jacko put it out in time, but Garnet's got no eyelashes no more.'

He and Garnet were living in an abandoned terrace house in Surry Hills with a bunch of other alternative lifestylers. One of these days the developers would torch it and they'd all go up in smoke.

'Developers,' I said. 'Or kids having fun. They're always setting derros alight. You're getting paranoid. Why would anyone be after you?'

He swallowed and looked around to see if anyone were hiding in my living room. 'I seen them, that's why.'

'Seen... saw what?'

'Seen a coupla blokes talkin last night.'

I got a picture in my head of Les propped up against a wall cuddling a bottle of muscatel in a brown paper bag.

'So?'

'So the bloke in the jeans give the bloke in the suit a bag...'

'What sort of a bag?'

'One of them briefcase things,' he said testily. He didn't like being interrupted when he was starting to hit his stride. 'The geezer in the suit looks in the bag, then they start arguin', then he shoots him.'

'What? Who shoots who, whom?'

'The copper shoots the bloke in the jeans.'

'You didn't say anything about cops before! What makes you think he was a cop?'

He laughed. 'I've seen a lot of coppers in me day, son.'

I digested this. It could be good or bad news, depending on which cop we were dealing with. And what was in the bag.

'Did he kill him?'

'Looked pretty dead to me.'

'So how come he's looking for you?'

'Because I took off like a flamin rocket, but I fell over and he heard me. I thought I heard him comin after me. Jesus.' He started to shake at the memory.

'You think he got a good look at you?'

'Must of.'

If he were a cop it would be easy for him to track down all the winos in the area. The poor old bastard was genuinely frightened. He hardly ever bit me for anything, so I made up a bed on the sofa for him and went back to sleep.

When I dragged out about eight, he was sitting at the kitchen table drinking beer and reading the paper. He looked even dirtier in the light. 'Have you told anyone else about this?' I asked.

'Shit no,' he said, but he looked shifty and I knew he was lying. If he had really witnessed a killing, he could be in danger and so could his friends.

'Come on, Les, who did you tell?'

'Garnet,' he admitted finally. 'Garnet Grahame.'

'Who's this Garnet?' I asked. 'And where did he get that weird name?'

'He comes from Queensland,' said Les, as if that explained it.

I gave up. 'Look, are you sure you didn't imagine all this?' I asked, hoping against hope.

He was offended and sulked into his beer. He was even more outraged when I told him he'd have to take a bath if he wanted to stay at my place. When he stomped off to the bathroom, I opened all the windows, then walked along the road to an early opener and bought him a flagon of wine. I had the usual rat cheese, half a tomato and bread with whiskers in the fridge, but I only bought some fresh bread and ham. I had a suspicion Les wasn't all that particular about food.

I hardly recognised him when he emerged from the bathroom with snow white hair and beard. 'Aren't you just a dear old soul,' I taunted.

'Piss off,' he said, but his eyes lit up when he saw the grog.

I had to go out but told him I'd ask around and see what was happening at the squat. It might be worth checking up on Garnet, too. He promised me he wouldn't leave the flat.

Les's squat was off South Dowling Street, one of a row of dilapidated terrace houses scheduled for redevelopment. Graffitists had made their bid for immortality with two-metre high tags. I climbed in through a broken window. Something, probably a rat, ran across my foot, the adrenalin surged and I suppressed a desire to scream.

Footsteps reverberating eerily, I picked my way carefully around the holes in the floor. Old squatters' cooking fires had scarred the floorboards and blackened the ceilings. The place was a death trap. It was also empty. I decided to try Belmore Park, a hangout near Central Station.

It was insufferably hot and stuffy as the city sweltered under a temperature inversion. The stink of car exhausts was overpowering. I parked the car in a loading zone and dodged through the clogged traffic and entered the park. It didn't take long to find a clump of winos around a flagon. With the usual ancients, a couple of teenage desperadoes were serving their apprenticeship in hopelessness. Two battle-scarred scarecrows circled each other throwing useless punches at the air.

When they finally registered my presence, they stared at me, muttering suspiciously, and one began to swear. I hunkered down next to a bloke who seemed slightly *compos mentis* and asked about Garnet.

'Garnet,' he said. 'Fuckin Garnet, ya say. Fuckin crazy name. Whaddya want with fuckin Garnet, ya bastard?'

'I'm a friend of Les's. Les wants to talk to him. Is any of you Garnet?'

'Nah. Can't ya see he's not here, ya stupid bastard.'

I had an overpowering urge to crack their heads together like coconuts but I persevered: 'Do you know where he is?'

It was too late. I'd lost them. A half-hearted fight had broken out over the flagon, with the usual streams of obscenities. I gave up. If Garnet were around, he'd probably return to the squat to sleep. I'd have to go back when it got dark.

Safe in the Valiant I turned on the radio to see if there had been a shooting the night before. Nothing.

Besides the usual envelopes with windows and a few new dust balls waiting in my office, there was a phone message from Lizzie inviting me to the opera; she had free tickets. She'd have to pay me.

The next news bulletin informed me that a twenty-six year old man had been found shot in a vacant lot in Surry Hills. They weren't releasing his name till his relatives had been contacted.

I rang Lizzie. After I'd told her she'd have to pay me to go to the opera, and she'd called me the usual names, I asked her if she knew anything about the Surry Hills victim.

'Yes, it's just come in. Male caucasian twenty-six, Joseph Fayyad, aka Joey Fay, company director of St Mary's. In other words, a Lebanese crim, probably a drug dealer. He's got some form — armed robbery. The *Tele* will probably call it a gangland slaying.'

'Is anyone helping the police with their inquiries?'

'Not that I know of. What's your interest, anyway?'

'I just might be harbouring a witness,' I said, and told her what Les had seen.

'Christ! Does anyone else know?'

'I think some derro friend of Les's called Garnet was either there too, or Les told him about it after. Somebody tried to set the poor old bastard alight. Les is sure they were after him.'

'You don't think it's just the usual psychopaths torching tramps?'

'I don't know. But I haven't been able to locate this famous Garnet yet. He could be hiding out but he might be stupid or drunk or desperate enough to go back to the squat tonight. I'll have a look, then I'll chuck it in. Anyway, it's going to be rough enough hiding Les in my flat without one of his mates along for the ride.'

'Watch your step. If the cops are mixed up in this, they'll be out combing the bushes for Garnet and Les. And they've got better resources than you.'

Before I hung up Lizzie asked: 'What sort of name is Garnet?'

'Queensland,' I said enigmatically.

I rang my flat and got no answer, but Les might have been too scared to answer the phone. Or out to it. I decided to check on him.

Something felt odd as soon as I got out of the lift. Then I realised what it was, there was a draught in the usually airless hallway. The hair on my neck reaching for the sky, I crept along the hall and stopped dead. My front door was ajar.

I don't regard myself as a coward, but I wasn't wildly enthusiastic about the prospect of interrupting a strung-out Darlo denizen with a knife. Or a rogue cop looking for a witness.

I told myself it was just Les being careless; besides, I couldn't stand out here forever like a garden gnome. Kicking the door wide open, I dropped low and peered in. A chair and the coffee table were overturned as if someone had fallen against them or kicked them out of the way, but the portable TV was still there. That meant it wasn't junkies. There was no sign of Les, apart from some empties.

The shrill peal of the telephone in the silence shot me in the back, and I jumped. When I answered it, no one was there.

Though I was beginning to get a bad feeling about this case, I wasn't ready to panic yet. Les could easily have gone out to find more grog: he could be anywhere. He could even be back at the park with his mates by now.

It was four o'clock and fear had sharpened my appetite, so I picked up the afternoon paper and walked a couple of blocks to Una's coffee lounge in Victoria Street and chewed my way through a huge plate of wiener schnitzel with refried potatoes. Una's was only half full; the art students, ex-cons living in furnished rooms, and writers and film makers who liked to live close to their subjects would start to come in for dinner about six.

The paper didn't tell me any more than Lizzie had. Outside the heat was building up, the black clouds had rolled in and the air was full of the sulphur smell that precedes rain. Despite all the aversion therapy I'd undergone in this case, I was dying for a beer.

With a couple of cold ales in Woolloomooloo as an incentive, I joined the rush and cut through Potts Point and the Cross. Now that I was looking for Les I noticed how many groups of boozers hung out in the area.

All the squatters in the vacant lot behind the railway station in Victoria Street were black; he wasn't among the the revellers playing guitars, singing tunelessly and obstructing the entrance to the subway in Darlinghurst Road; there were only homeless kids, marauding chickenhawks and tourists in Fitzroy Gardens; and the little park under the railway overpass in Forbes Street was empty.

The pubs were filling up with workers from the Navy dockyard and locals from the public housing estate escaping from cramped terrace houses and flats. The rock and roll was too loud in the Woolloomooloo Bay, so I went to The Bells. Resisting the pink painters, it remained militantly working class. Most of the dispirited patrons stayed glued to the telly and I was left alone to worry in peace.

If Les had gone on a bender in the Cross, I figured he'd probably gravitate to the nearby Matthew Talbot Hostel to sleep it off, so I stopped in and asked.

A sallow youth dressed in black and the regulation Doc Martens guarded the desk. When I asked him about Les and Garnet, he dragged himself away from his magazine long enough to tell me in a bored voice that he couldn't release personal details about clients.

Maybe it was the heat: I snapped. Grabbing him by the tee shirt, I jerked him to his feet and said: 'It must be hard looking cool with a face full of pimples. Let me get rid of a few of them for you.'

'He's not here,' he bit out. He'd perked up considerably: fear is a reliable antidote for boredom.

I dropped him back into his chair and left. He aimed a few bad words at my back but I pretended he'd missed. Time for a tour of the Sydney the Japanese never see.

Derro territory takes in the part of Surry Hills the hairdressers, legal aid lawyers and media types haven't gentrified. One pocket of old Surry Hills centres on Campbell Street, near Central Station. Remnants of the Chinese community cling to the area, but it is dominated by the new police headquarters, Sydney City Mission's Swanton Lodge, the Salvation Army Men's Home and some private doss houses.

The winos had moved in on the cops when they'd landscaped the grounds of their new palace of justice. The little park is close to free food and shelter when it gets cold and the police presence protects them from drugged-out muggers and derro bashers. I had some success with the group of merrymakers who'd settled in for the day: they knew Les and Garnet but said they hadn't seen either of them since yesterday.

Tree-lined Campbell street was deserted and littered. A hot wind chased cans, chip packets and paper cups by me as I walked down past an Indonesian language Anglican church, the Australian Chinese Community Association, some dingy, failing shops, travel agents and a couple of picture framers to Foster Street, where about thirty men were hanging around outside the Salvation Army Men's Home.

Home was a warm word for what turned out to be a gloomy, red-brick building at the end of a rubbish-strewn alley. There an old bloke in a battered, filthy tweed suit, a bankrobber's beanie and two-toned platform shoes told me he'd been at the squat the night before when the arsonist had struck, and he thought Garnet had said something about pissing off to the Cross.

Time to revisit the squat. A flicker of light through the front window told me someone was in residence. I knew if I knocked or called out they'd all clear out through the back, so I went in through the window. When I loomed over them, they tried to collect themselves to scatter. Les wasn't there.

'I'm a friend of Les's, I yelled. 'I'm looking for Les and Garnet. Is Garnet here?'

They mumbled and shuffled around and finally someone said: 'He's not here. We aint seen Garnet since last night. He took off when that bastard...' He tapered off into an obscene tirade.

I was trying to ask them where Garnet might have gone when the front door fell in with an almighty crash. The tramps scattered like chooks before the axe, and I tried to follow them out a back window.

'Stop or we'll shoot!' roared a voice and we turned into blinding torchlight. There were two of them and they'd done this before. Coppers. For once the arrival of the cavalry didn't cheer me up.

'Up against the wall!' ordered a young voice over the frightened babbling. I hung low, just out of the torch beam. Deciding the bums were taking too long, a cop grabbed one of the more sober looking of our little group and banged his head against the wall.

'Leave him alone, you bastard!' I shouted. 'You'll kill him!'

Both torches swung onto me. There was a surprised silence, and the victim, forgotten, fell down with blood gushing from his head. It didn't take the older cop long to collect his wits. 'Who the fuck are you and what are you doing here?' he roared. I couldn't see his face because of the light in my eyes, but I could tell he was in charge. The young punk came over, put the torch under my chin and said: 'You heard the man. Who are you?'

'I'm a private investigator,' I said.

'ID,' he barked, and I got out my licence.

He threw it to the boss cop, who examined it out and said quietly: 'And just what might you be investigating here?'

'I'm looking for a runaway kid. I'm checking out the squats.'

They caucused briefly, decided I hadn't broken any laws, and told me to get lost. Warning us to put out the fires and leave, they backed out, keeping the torches high, and drove off with a scream of taxpayers' tyres.

I was a bit shaken by the random violence, but the derros were used to it: it was part of their cost of living. They had a snort to quieten their nerves, then helped me put their wounded mate in the Valiant. I dropped him off at St Vincent's casualty, but his memory lingered on for weeks on the car's upholstery.

It could be pure coincidence—first an attempted murder, now a police bust at the squat—but it could mean trouble for Les. I'd have to find him.

The receding tide of adrenalin made me hungry, so I picked up two hamburgers on my way home. Then I opened a Heineken and turned on the TV. A perfect, poised, plastic blond newsreader told me that the shooting of Joseph Fayyad had taken a dramatic turn. I couldn't decide whether it was a turn for the better or worse.

About a minute later, Lizzie rang. 'Christ, did you see the news?'

'Yeah. I didn't like it.' Then I told her about my latest brush with the law.

She digested that and said: 'I think we've got to take Les out of circulation. Before they do.'

'How?'

'We've got to dry him out and disappear him. As long as he's a drunk, he's in danger. The booze will drag him back on the streets pretty soon. And he won't be able to stay away from his mates. The cops only have to wait him out.'

'I don't know how to dry him out. I have enough trouble with myself.'

'What about some sort of institution? Don't they have places to dry people out?'

'Yeah, but you have to volunteer. They won't keep anybody there against their will any more.'

'Maybe you can scare him into it.'

'Maybe. But he'll pretty soon forget how scared he was when the snakes start crawling on him.'

'What about the Catholics? They must have some san for Catholic drunks somewhere. And they wouldn't give a bugger about keeping someone there against their will. Not unless they've changed a lot since my time.'

'Declan Doherty,' I said. 'He'll know.'

The storm broke just as I hung up. It started with hail, then the rain came down in buckets. Storms calm me down, so I stood at my open window watching the lightning flash over the city till the water started to come in. It wouldn't be much fun sleeping out tonight.

It was too late to call the priest at his North Sydney convent, so I had another beer and fell into bed.

The following day dawned clear and innocent. The storm had washed away some of Sydney's sins: the city shone. As soon as I figured the nuns were back from morning mass, I hassled them into calling Fr Doherty to the phone. I swore him to secrecy and gave him enough information to intrigue him but not enough to put Les in danger; he knew too many cops and too many people who drank with cops.

His answer was the St John of God Psychiatric Hospital at Richmond.

'Christ, he's not crazy,' I protested. 'Not yet.'

He told me the hospital was run by Brother Gerry Rafferty, who had been for a time the toast of the Sydney media with his trenchant criticisms of the church's social policies.

'Not the dreaded sin of pride?' I asked.

'The same,' said the priest drily.

Apparently the Cardinal, a short-back-and-sides conservative, had eventually run out of patience and employed the Russian solution for political dissenters — exile.

'Rafferty is a good man,' the priest reassured me. 'Very human. Your friend will be safe with him.'

He said he'd try to tee it up with Rafferty and get back to me. I tried to thank him for his help, but he cut me short: 'Les O'Rourke was a very good footballer in his time. It would be a pity to see the grog get the better of him.'

I waited by the phone reading the paper. It rang twice but nobody answered when I picked it up. Maybe an admirer had written my number in the Ladies at Kings Cross railway station. Suddenly my gut clenched. Hidden among the one-paragraph grabs was an item about a transient who'd been washed into a storm drain and drowned the night before. His name was Garnet Grahame.

Now I really had to find Les. I lost more of the lining of my stomach while I waited for the priest to call back. When he came through, I told him he'd get his reward in heaven; he said that was fine, as long as there was a film society and a decent coffee shop.

As soon as the door closed behind me, the phone rang again. Feeling as though I were trapped in a re-run of *The Exterminating Angel*, I hesitated, then burst back into the flat. This time it was Les.

Relief made me angry. 'Where the fuck have you been, you old bastard. I've been combing the city looking for you.'

'Jesus, mate. I've been tryin ta phone ya, but the bloody phones keep eatin me thirty cents.'

'Where are you?'

'I'm in a boardin house in South Dowling Street.'

'What happened? Why did you leave?'

'I was lookin out the window of your place and I seen the cops pull up outside, so I took off down the stairs. Nearly bloody died of fright.'

'I suppose you shut the door after you?'

A guilty silence. 'Well, I dunno, mate, now you mention it. I might not of. I was in a bit of a hurry.'

'Have you heard the news?'

'No, mate. I've been stayin in me room. What's goin on?'

'The bloke that was killed was a Lebanese drug dealer. His girlfriend has come forward and accused Mike McNicholl of killing him. She says they'd set up a meeting in that vacant lot so Fayyad could hand over a hundred grand to McNicholl. Now Fayyad's dead and the money's disappeared.'

There was a silence on the other end of the line. 'Do you know who McNicholl is?' I asked.

'Nah, but if he was the cop I seen with the gun, he's bad news.'

'Bad news is not half of it. He's a very senior cop, Les, very well connected. Been decorated for bravery several times. Likes killing people.'

'Shit. So what are we gunna do?'

'We're going to take you out of circulation.'

'How?'

'Look, Les, as long as you're on the piss, you're in danger. The cops only have to keep watching the places where the winos hang out, and eventually they'll pick you up. Then you'll have an accident, or they'll fill you up with hundred proof and it'll kill you. Do you understand what I'm saying?'

'Yeah, mate. But I dunno if I can give it up...'

It seemed I had to use it: 'One more thing, Les. Garnet is dead. He fell in a storm drain and drowned last night. Near Moore Park.'

There was a silence filled with fear, or grief or both.

'Are you all right, mate?' I asked.

'Yeah, I'm all right.' His tone told me he'd conceded.

'OK, pack your swag and I'll pick you up in half an hour.'

I hardly recognised the respectable old party waiting for me at Country Trains: it was an unusually clean and subdued Les. He was wearing a pale blue polyester leisure suit, a wide batik tie and a hunted look. And he'd aged; all the manic energy had gone, sweated out with the alcohol.

I bought him sandwiches, fruit cake and a couple of chocolate bars and we sat about uneasily in those last embarrassing minutes before departure. Rafferty had engineered a reconciliation between the old man and his widowed sister, and Les was moving to Dubbo.

I warned him to keep off the grog and keep his mouth shut and stay out of the cops' line of fire: 'They all went to the academy together, and they're as thick as thieves. Don't trust any of them.'

He assured me he was dry and that he was going to be a perfect senior citizen and take up bowls. I had my doubts, but I couldn't keep him in protective custody forever. That was Ida's job now.

Forgetting for a moment that the only males allowed to show affection are footballers, poofters and reffos, I tried to give Les a hug when the time came to board. Surprised, he leapt backwards, gave me a sort of pat and bolted. The train pulled out and a part of my history went with it.

I watched the Fayyad murder case unfold. McNicholl walked. Fayyad's girlfriend slid deeper into drugs and trouble and was eventually fished out of the pond in Centennial Park.

Sometimes when I see McNicholl's picture in the papers or read the latest police corruption headlines, I wonder if I really saved Les from death by violence or simply death by cirrhosis.

Loco Parentis

Professor David Granger was a successful academic and might even have been a good scholar. He certainly looked the part — a sensitive, intelligent face, thick hair greying glamorously, and excellent tweeds. The TV talk shows loved him.

I disliked him on sight and caught myself looking for some secret, nasty flaw.

'I've come about my daughter, Mr Fish,' he said, glancing nervously around my humble professional suite. He had an actor's voice, polished on thousands of podiums. It must have sent shivers down history students' spines over the years as he pontificated about the Hanseatic League or the Holy Roman Empire.

I waited while he took in the dying aspidistra, the battered filing cabinets and my Save Bondi Beach poster.

'Your daughter?' I prompted.

'Ah, she seems to have disappeared from the house she shares with some other students.'

'Disappeared?' I asked. 'Does than mean you think she didn't leave of her own free will?'

'I don't know. We've always kept in touch, but the last time I rang the house they said she'd left suddenly and nobody seems to know where she's gone. I've called all our relatives and friends. Nothing. It's completely out of character for her to be irresponsible.

'How old is she?'

'Claire's twenty.'

'Lots of twenty-year-old girls don't tell their parents where they're going,' I said. 'Especially if they don't live at home.'

He bridled slightly. 'I'm quite aware of that, Mr Fish, but I like to think we're very close.'

He saw my expression and said: 'I know most parents say that, but in our case it's true.'

'Is she close to her mother too?'

'My wife Louise died five years ago. I've brought Claire up by myself.'

'Has anything upset her lately?'

'Not that I know of,' he said, but he'd hesitated a fraction too long. Like Granger's, my job involved searching for the truth, and I knew immediately a grain of it lay in that small silence.

'Is Claire the kind of girl who can look after herself?' I asked.

'She's very... vulnerable. Too sensitive, perhaps. She has a tendency to brood, to make mountains out of molehills. Her mother was the same. Louise's death hit Claire very hard but she seemed to be getting over it, especially since she started university and made some new friends. Then this...'

He stared off into the distance, remembering his wife, perhaps, but I couldn't read his face. Some men find sensitive women romantic; others feel more like slapping it out of them. By the end of the case I'd probably know which description fitted the professor, but so far I hadn't got past his public face.

He came back to the present and said: 'I suppose the answer to your question is no. My daughter is not terribly well equipped for the real world.'

'Money?' I asked.

He gave me a shocked look.

'Not for me,' I said, patiently. 'Does she have any money of her own?'

He was relieved. Mean, too, I thought.

'She'll come into a trust fund from her mother when she turns twenty one. In the meantime, I give her an allowance, and she has credit cards and access to a joint account.'

'Has she taken any large sums out of the account?'

'No. Not a cent. And she doesn't seem to be using her cards.'

So a sensitive, unworldly girl was on the loose somewhere with no money. It was beginning to look more interesting than the usual runaway daughter shacked up with Mr Wrong or hitting the nightspots in search of prohibited substances and bad company.

I was even more intrigued when he showed me a photograph of Claire Granger. She was lovely — tragic looking, like a consumptive in a Victorian novel. She had her father's bones, but someone else's enormous yellow-brown eyes fringed with long thick dark lashes, dead white skin and thick blue-black hair pulled back like a ballet dancer.

'She's beautiful,' I said.

He didn't like a lowlife private dick harbouring lascivious thoughts about his pride and joy; she had been bred for better things. The charm ebbed slightly, uncovering a more believable petulance. But he needed me, so he only said: 'She's like her mother.'

As I drove out to the student house in Newtown, I thought about the money angle. It could mean a number of things. If someone had kidnapped the girl, he would have made a demand by now, or he could have forced the girl to take the money out of her account. If she'd simply run away, she could have a job, or some boyfriend could be keeping her. In that case, her refusal to use her father's money and her silence flatly contradicted Granger's rosy picture of their relationship.

Newtown was its charming old self — litter, dog shit, vandalised telephones, stumbling derros cherishing brown paper bags, aggressive Samoans hurtling out of pubs, unbreathable air and non-stop traffic.

Despite the fond hopes of some of its newer inhabitants, Newtown was not going to be another Paddington until they rerouted the traffic and put in some parks and the rich gays transformed the bloodbath pubs into beer boutiques, but there were signs of change. Hopeful yuppies had gentrified some of the streets and I spotted trendy restaurants and junque shops, Vietnamese bakeries and even a few bookshops. The food was still the best and cheapest in Sydney, so I did a quick deli raid while I had the chance.

The house was the usual student terrace with a leprous-looking frangipani, some struggling grass and a couple of garbage bags decorating the mean front yard. I knocked on the door and a dog barked shrilly and hurled itself against the door. I cursed: I am not a dog lover. There are almost as many dogs as cockroaches in Newtown, and they shit more.

The door was answered by a nervous gangly youth trying to disguise his Cranbrook background with a black punk costume and dirty bare feet. The dog was the regulation ugly student bitser who took its job far too seriously. It tried to jump on me, but the boy grabbed its collar and said: 'Down, Simon!'

'Simon?' I inquired. The look on my face made the boy blush, which made him dislike me immediately. I should learn to keep my face shut.

I told him I was there on behalf of Claire Granger's father, so he let me in and told me his name was Matthew. I asked if I could look around. He didn't dare refuse but lurked by Claire's bedroom door while I poked about to make sure I didn't steal anything or masturbate on her teddy bear.

The wardrobe was still full of black nineties clothes, which meant she had left in a hurry, intended to return, or wouldn't need them where she was going. She'd also left expensive perfumes, makeup, nicknacks and family photos on the old mahogany dressing table.

'Did she say anything to you about leaving?' I asked the boy.

'No.'

'Did she pay the rent before she left?'

'Professor Granger pays the rent for her, and it's paid up till the end of term.'

'What do you think happened to her?' I asked.

He shrugged. 'Maybe she needed some space.'

'How did she get along with her father?'

'He pays for everything, takes her out to eat, she goes home a lot. I suppose they get on OK.'

'Did she ever talk about him?'

'No.'

The kid wasn't going out of his way to help, but maybe he disliked Granger as much as I did.

I inventoried the room: plenty of clothes, hard to tell if any were gone or not; no personal papers; a silver-framed picture of the girl and her father looking happy. A girl who loved her daddy would have taken that picture with her, surely?

'Does her father visit her here?' I asked.

'He used to, then he stopped.'

'When?'

'About three months ago.'

'Why, did they have a fight?'

'If they did, they didn't do it in front of me,' he said.

'Who else lives here?' I asked.

'Miranda.'

'Where can I find Miranda?'

'She's out prac teaching today I think. She'll probably be home about four thirty.'

Just then the front door slammed. Simon barked in joyous welcome, and was told to shut up by a high-pitched cultivated voice. Feet thundered up the stairs and stopped, and I found myself caught in the surprised sapphire stare of Miranda Marshall.

Miranda was a tall, well-built girl with a perfect rosy complexion and white blond hair. Her eyebrows and lashes were blond and she wore no makeup. She looked like a milkmaid, but those feet had never squelched through cowshit, nor had those white hands ever done a day's hard work.

She shot a glance at Matthew who quickly warned: 'He's a private detective.'

The milkmaid's pale eyebrows rose and the pink mouth formed a silent Oh!

'Professor Granger sent me here because he's worried about Claire,' I explained.

There was a deathly silence. 'Are you her friend?' I asked.

'I'm her best friend,' said the girl. 'We went to school together.'

'Do you know what's happened to her?'

'No. Well, she... It's not...', she looked to Matthew for help, but he was avoiding her eye.

'If she's your best friend, how come she didn't tell you where she was going?'

The girl flushed. 'I don't know.'

'Has she ever done this sort of thing before? Gone off in the middle of term without telling anyone?'

'No, of course not.'

'Aren't you worried?'

'Of course I'm worried. But I don't know anything!'

'Claire is your best friend, you've known her all your life and you don't know why she's run away without telling her father where she's going?' I hammered.

I was being a tough guy, but these two were playing some sort of game, and it was time to break it up. Her pretty face crumpled and she burst into tears and rushed into her room.

'When you decide to talk, call me.' I yelled after her before the bedroom door slammed.

Matthew scowled at me and went after the girl, so I let myself out. The mutt heard me coming, set up a ferocious barking, pelted down the hall and launched itself at me. I dodged sideways quickly in a manoeuvre perfected too many years ago in the second thirteen at Marist Brothers Darlinghurst. The dog missed me, and skidded down the lino. Making sure the coast was clear, I booted it firmly up the arse — mutt cutlet.

Feeling more cheerful than I had for hours, I let myself out before the dog's outraged yelps brought the wrath of the Newtown chapter of Animal Liberation down on my head.

That afternoon I called Granger and took a taxi to Sydney University and the Mungo McCallum Building, an ugly, boxlike sixties edifice, designed by some pretentious architect. I told the Professor I thought his daughter had left of her own free will, but that her housemates were either unwilling or unable to shed any light on her reasons.

He lit a pipe fussily, perhaps to give himself time to think, and said, too casually: 'Miranda didn't say anything?'

'No. She burst into tears and threw a tantrum, but I think that was designed to get rid of me.'

'Miranda is a very highly-strung girl,' he said. 'Very highly-strung.'

'Really?' I said. Next he'd tell me she was suffering from nerves. 'I think she knows something she doesn't want to tell me. Perhaps the girls had a fight. If they're very close, that could have upset Claire enough to make her move out.'

'What would they fight about?' he asked.

Nobody could be that naive. 'A man, of course. What else do women ever fight about?'

'Claire has never mentioned a man to me,' he said, sounding put out. The professor had a lot to learn about women, and even more about parenting.

This line of inquiry wasn't going anywhere, so I asked him if Claire had any other friends. Preferably someone who wasn't playing games.

'Rosie Blake,' he said, his mouth turning down as if he'd bitten on something sour. A bad influence? A state school product?

Rosie Blake was one of Granger's students so I could catch her after his two o'clock lecture.

Killing time, I took a walk around the campus, marvelling at how quiet, clean and unreal it was, and how healthy, purposeful and amiable its inmates were. I had a surge of nostalgia for the sixties, when the universities had reared up, like dying dinosaurs, for one mad burst of life before slipping back into their characteristic coma.

All the noise in the country seemed to be coming from failed beer barons and right wing Labor apparatchiks, I thought sourly as I poked around in the bookstore. The students were too busy working towards their first BMW and a $350,000 house to worry about politics anymore, but I wondered what academics did with all that spare time they swore they didn't have because they were so busy giving the country intellectual and moral leadership.

As I'm fortunately not in the business of providing any sort of leadership, I wasted a couple of pleasant hours in the Wentworth Building eating health food and watching the parade of milk-fed nubile girls taking time out between childhood and parenthood. I felt older than a refugee from Shangri-La.

Then I sat in on Granger's lecture. He was good—humorous, fluent, magnetic on the stage. I was dealing with a fine actor here, which added just one more complication to the case.

He'd asked Rosie Blake to stay behind. She turned out to be a large, lively girl with beautiful olive skin, bright knowing eyes and punked orange hair. Her arms jangled with silver bangles and each ear sported several earrings.

Rosie wasn't the least awed by Professor Granger, whose obvious disapproval made her smirk. 'Isn't he a right royal pain in the arse?' she said to me as he walked away.

'He's my client,' I said.

'Lucky you,' she said with a laugh that brought Bette Midler to mind.

We repaired to a coffee shop and I told her what was going on.

'I'm not surprised she's gone,' said Rosie. 'She's been really depressed for a couple of months.'

'What about?'

'Is it any of your business?'

'Granger think it's his business and that makes it mine,' I said. 'His daughter is missing, she doesn't have any money, and he wants her found.'

'What if she doesn't want to be found?'

'I'll find her anyway,' I said. 'That's what I'm getting paid for. You might as well make it a bit easier for me.'

She laughed. 'You're all right. No bullshit. But Granger's a total phony. I don't trust him and I'm glad Claire's got out from under his thumb.'

'What do you mean?'

'I suppose you know Claire's mother died a few years ago. Well, Granger insisted on looking after Claire by himself, and he's turned her into a real daddy's girl. It's not healthy. He makes my flesh creep.'

'I would have thought the girls would have gone for him...'

'Oh they do, they do, believe me. But he's got this amazing ego. Women are just grist for the mill. He doesn't give a stuff about them, really; it's just the thrill of conquest.'

'So he plays around with his students.'

'Yeah. And Claire picked that up pretty fast when she got onto campus. I think it was a big shock. She'd believed he was a saint, and that she was the only woman in his life.'

'A big enough shock to make her run away?'

'No. Something else happened a couple of months ago. Claire found out that her mother didn't die in a car accident; she killed herself.'

'How did she find out?'

'Some old friend of her mother's came back from America and looked Claire up. It just slipped out. The woman didn't know Claire hadn't been told. Claire was terribly upset, but the damage was done. She thought her father should have told her the truth. She was practically hysterical and wouldn't get out of bed for days.'

'Did Miranda look after her?'

Rosie's eyes widened and her eyebrows went up. 'Miranda?! You've got to be joking!'

'How well do you know Miranda?' I asked.

'Well enough.'

'Did you meet her here with Claire?'

'God, no. Miranda's too stupid to keep up with Claire academically. She's doing something called Early Childhood Education. It's just kindergarten teaching really. If you ask me, it's an inspired choice. Miranda is like a big pink baby herself—manipulative and absolutely determined to her own way. I don't know if she lies on the floor and screams and drums her heels, but it wouldn't surprise me.'

'So why the great friendship with Claire?'

'Claire's parents sent her to one of those awful schools for stupid hearty girls who marry well, and Miranda probably seemed like the best of a bad bunch. Miranda prides herself on her sensitivity, you know, and she's a great actress. Maybe Claire fell for it and it just stuck. It takes years to shake off some of the dags you knew at school.'

'But she's started making new friends here?'

'Yeah, me. I'm the real world. Her old man hates me because he can see I think he's a deadshit, and he's afraid I'll corrupt Claire's vowels.'

And that's not all, I thought.

Her laugh boomed out, and several young men turned to look and kept staring. Rosie wasn't beautiful, but she had an elemental force that would corrupt a curate.

'Tell me about Claire, Rosie. What goes on in her head?'

The girl became serious, and said: 'Damaged, in a word. Her mother depended on her too much because she was lonely and disappointed. Then Granger tried to take her over after her mother died, for revenge I think. Hell, I'm no psychologist. But Claire has everything — looks, brains, money; she's even nice, for God's sake — but she's got no confidence.

'And I think her mother made her a bit strange about men, probably filled her ears with tales of what brutes they are. I don't think she's really been out with a man since I've known her. It's not fair. She should be happy.'

'Was there some sort of trouble between Miranda and Claire?'
'Why?'
'When I went around to the house and tried to talk to her, she threw a scene and ran off.'

'Sounds like a guilty conscience to me,' said Rosie.
'Were they fighting over a man?' I asked.
'You could put it that way,' said Rosie delphically and refused to elaborate.

I asked Rosie the name of Claire's mother's friend, but all she knew was that the woman was married to some American government official who'd just been posted to Australia.

'If you remember anything important, give me a call,' I said, handing her my business card.

'I'm not going to tell you anything more, but I might get in touch one rainy night,' she said, giving me a smile that let me back into Shangri-La. Thank heaven for little girls, or in this case, big ones.

A quick phone call to Lizzie Darcy got me the name of Louise Granger's friend, and another couple secured me an interview with Elaine Shumway in Canberra.

I took the Valiant to Canberra because the road is fast and the flight too short to get a drink on, and it gave me time to play my new Zydeco tape and mull over the case. Whatever Claire had learned about her mother's death had upset her, but that hadn't made her bolt. I was convinced Miranda was behind it all, but I was just as sure David Granger wasn't playing a straight bat.

Elaine Shumway was about forty five with green eyes as pale as river water and expensive tawny hair. Her even tan and well-muscled body advertised tennis, and she was dressed in something olive green that reeked of New York. Her gold bracelet would have bought me a one-bedroom apartment in Darlinghurst. She made Rosie look like a barmaid.

Mrs Shumway told me she'd been an American high school exchange student who'd stayed with Louise's family, and had kept in touch by letter over the years. When Louise married Granger they'd honeymooned in the States and the women had renewed their friendship.

I told her about Claire's disappearance and said I was almost certain Louise's suicide had had something to do with it. Did she know why Louise had killed herself?

'Louise was a sensitive, vulnerable girl, and she grew into an unhappy woman. She didn't have much resilience.'

'Was she neurotic?'

'Put it this way: if she'd married the right sort of man she would have coped.'

'And Granger wasn't?'

'You've met him?'

'Yes.'

'What do you think of him?'

'Handsome, smooth, clever. Also vain, probably selfish and very guarded. If there's a real person in there, I haven't met him yet.'

She looked at me with a new respect. 'I think you've caught the essential David,' she said drily. 'He is also a compulsive womaniser. He was unfaithful to Louise right from the start. She wasn't very confident to begin with, and David destroyed what little self-esteem she had.'

'Why didn't she leave him?'

'Louise was very strictly brought up. She thought their sort of people didn't get divorces. But she was also afraid he'd get custody of Claire. Louise had a nervous breakdown when Claire was a baby and ended up in a sanatorium. She thought David would use that to prove she was an unfit mother. They both doted on Claire.'

Louise Granger had put up with her husband's womanising for twenty years. If she loved her daughter so much, why did she kill herself when Claire was just becoming a woman, when the girl needed her most? There had to be something else.

'Did something push Claire Granger over the edge, Mrs Shumway, some incident?'

Elaine Shumway uncoiled from the couch and went to the window to look out at calm, beautiful, empty Forrest, and made up her mind to come clean. 'This is difficult for me, Mr Fish. Louise confided in me, and what I'm about to tell you could prove very damaging. To a number of a people. But I want you to find Claire and make sure she's all right, and it might help you.'

She returned to the couch and we waited while a maid served us coffee and French pastries. Then she said: 'The last letter I received from Louise was dated a few days before her death. She said she couldn't take any more. She was afraid it would all come out into the open and ruin Claire's life as well as her own...'

'The womanising?'

'Some people have another name for it, Mr Fish. David and Louise had a beach house—Louise owned it actually: she had the money—and Claire had asked one of her friends along for a week. Louise walked in on David and the girl in a somewhat compromising position. The girl was fourteen.'

'Did she say who the girl was?' I asked, becoming aware that the hair on the back of my neck was standing up. The case was coming together at last.

The woman paused to light a low-tar cigarette, took a long drag, and murmured: 'Miranda something or other, I believe.'

I thanked her and got up to leave. 'How are you finding Canberra, Mrs Shumway?' I asked.

'I'll let you know when I land,' she said, smiling sweetly, and closed the door on me.

Driving along Mugga Way through the privileged, sleeping suburbs back to the comforting noise and pollution of Sydney, I thought about Miranda. I'd seen her as a good actress when in fact she was incapable of acting at all. It was time to return to Newtown.

Next morning I parked nearby and waited till Matthew had left, then went and knocked on the door. The mutt started up, and Miranda's head appeared over the balcony. She ducked back quickly, but I'd seen her. 'Go away or I'll call the police!' she yelled.

'Open the fucking door or I'll kick it down,' I warned. It wouldn't have taken much; it was so weathered you could see through some of the cracks into the hall.

There was a prolonged pause, then Miranda opened the door, flushed, blond and very fetching in a fluffy dressing gown.

I pushed past her and sat down on the lumpy couch. 'Seduced any professors lately?' I asked.

She gave a small shriek and tried to run past me up the stairs. I snaked out an arm, caught her easily round the waist and frog-marched her back to an armchair.

'I'll scream rape!' she threatened.

'With your record, it won't stick,' I said.

She glared and pursed her lips.

'OK,' I said. 'Let's hear it. What happened between you and Claire?'

'It was just a quarrel over a man,' said the girl.

'You mean she found out you've been having it off with her father for the past five years?'

She flushed scarlet: 'Who told you that?'

'Louise's best friend,' I said.

'She hasn't told Claire, has she?' whispered the girl.

'No, you're in luck.'

'I swear Claire doesn't know that,' said Miranda. 'Someone at uni told her they'd seen us together, that's all, and she was very upset.'

'When did all this happen?'

'Just before she ran away.'

'But it all started a couple of months before that, didn't it, when she stopped calling her father?'

'She found out that Louise hadn't died in an accident; she'd killed herself by driving the car into a tree. Claire thought it was her father's fault and that he'd lied to her to cover up. So when she found out about David and me she went spare. She said David had taken everything from her. First her mother, and now her best friend. She said she didn't have anything left in the world.'

Except beauty, brains and loads of money, I thought uncharitably.

The girl was sobbing now. 'I'm terrified she's gone off and killed herself like her mother did. And it's all my fault. I'm so frightened.'

I wasn't exactly ecstatic either. 'Where would she go? Do you have any idea?'

'No. She wouldn't speak to me. She left while I was out. She didn't even leave a note for Matthew. And she left her dog here.'

I could understand that part of it, at least.

I sat and watched the girl cry for a while, wondering how I'd find Claire Granger. Australia is a big place. She could be working in a fish and chip shop at Kirribilli or waitressing in a Barrier Reef resort. I was pretty sure she wouldn't be flagging down strangers at the Cross.

'This is partly your fault,' I said to the snuffling Miranda as I left. 'You've got what you wanted but you've destroyed one woman and possibly two to get it. If you decide to start being a human being, rack your brains and come up with some ideas about where she's gone. You've known her all your life, use your imagination.'

I flicked her a card. 'And call me as soon as you have anything.'

Without eye makeup and with red eyes Miranda looked like a white cat, but as I don't like cats either, it didn't soften my heart.

I didn't bother talking to Granger. I knew Miranda would be on the phone to him the minute I left, and I didn't feel all that well disposed towards my client. Instead I rang Lizzie and took her to lunch at a German place in The Rocks and told her something about the case.

I was carrying on about Miranda when Lizzie silenced me with one of the looks that had got her fired from a TV current affairs show for being too hard on politicians and industrialists. 'Don't you think you're being a little unfair to Miranda? After all, she was seduced at fourteen by her best friend's father, someone in a position of trust. Fourteen is pretty young...'

'Maybe she wanted him to do it.'

'Don't be so... male! How can you know what Miranda was like before Granger got his hooks into her? If Miranda is a monster, Granger helped create her.'

Suitably chastened, I confessed I was worried about Claire. 'What if she's her mother's daughter?'

'She's David Granger's daughter too,' said Lizzie. 'And I'd tend to attribute him with fairly healthy survival instincts, wouldn't you?'

I had to agree.'

'If she'd killed herself, the body would have turned up by now, so she's probably hiding out somewhere, feeling wounded, waiting to be rescued.'

Lizzie is always worth the price of a meal, she's totally discreet and never panics.

'What did you think of Elaine Shumway?' she asked.

'Why?'

'Oh, she's much married, lots of money, old husband. I've heard she's cutting a swathe through Canberra.'

'I liked her,' I said. 'She had loads of class, looks like a million dollars and warned me exactly what I was up against.'

'I think you've fallen in love,' laughed Lizzie.

'Again,' I moaned.

A 'very, very urgent' phone message from Rosie Blake awaited me at the office.

'Something very weird has happened,' she told me when I called her at home. 'It might have something to do with Claire.'

'What?'

'This really strange guy went off his head in my English Literature tute today. Started crying, throwing things, wanting to fight everybody...'

'Yeah, but what's this got to do with Claire?'

'Gimme a chance, will ya! The tutor called the health service, and when they were trying to drag him out, he kept saying "I didn't mean to do it. I couldn't help myself. I'm sorry." stuff like that. Then I remembered he used to hang around Claire all the time. I wanted her to piss him off because he's such a creep, but she was too nice.'

'What's he like?

'A loser. Never washed, dirty clothes, green teeth, no friends. He used to talk about killing himself all the time.'

'Didn't anybody do anything about him?'

'No, of course not. Half the kids in English Lit are crazy as coots.'

I hadn't attended enough English tutorials at uni to get to know anybody, so I had to take her word for it: 'But is this kid really dangerous?'

'I don't know, but what if Claire didn't run away? What if this freak did something to her? She might be buried in his backyard. Girls do get murdered, you know.'

I knew. 'Does this person have a name?'

'Gary Jones.'

'Can I talk to him?'

'No, last I heard they'd shot him full of largactyl and taken him off to some psych hospital. I know where he lives though.'

'Where?'

'I'll tell you if you let me come along.'

'No.'

'Why not?'

'Break and enter wouldn't look too good on your CV.'

'Don't be so bourgeois!'

I changed tack: 'You want to help me dig up a body from the backyard? In this heat?'

That carried the day, but I had to promise to let her know immediately if I found anything suspicious.

Gary Jones, it turned out, rented a room in a terrace in one of the dreary back streets of Glebe. Nothing stirred in the street, not even a leaf. There weren't any leaves, in fact, or trees or flowers. Only concrete and the occasional dismantled motorbike chained to a front fence.

I went in through the back lane and entered via the laundry window. The kitchen was like a bomb site, littered with the debris of a hundred meals. Baked bean tins spilled out of a green garbage bag, milk curdled in cartons, weetbix had turned to concrete in bowls and dirty dishes overflowed the sink and festooned every flat surface. The stink was gut wrenching. My arrival stampeded a herd of napalm resistant cockroaches.

I pushed through into the musty living room, where blackout blankets barred most of the light, and almost blew an artery. On closer inspection the naked woman motionless in a chair in the gloom turned into a tailor's dummy. It was getting weirder.

When my blood pressure returned to normal, I mounted the stairs.

The first bedroom was your average male student cesspit with grey sheets and piles of mouldy socks and underwear and a tattered Midnight Oil poster on the wall.

The second bedroom achieved another level of alienation altogether. The walls and windows were painted black and I had to force open a window to stave off an attack of claustrophobia.

Lit by available light, the room revealed its first secret — a picture gallery. Claire was there, along with candid shots of about twenty other pretty girls.

Though the girls were much of an age, they came in all shapes and sizes. Why did they seem alike? Then it hit me: they had an innocent, unworldly air, the hesitant, unbudded look of girls who hadn't yet crossed some invisible line into womanhood. They might even have been virgins.

The shrill ringing of a phone downstairs gave me an adrenalin rush and cut short my musings about Gary Jones' tastes in women. Irrationally, I was certain the person on the other end knew I was there, trespassing, fingering some madman's fantasies, and I was paralysed till the phone stopped. Then I went through his desk. The camera was there, along with some bills and lots of notes on structuralism. No wonder he'd flipped. No letters or pictures of family or friends: nothing personal at all.

Now that the phone had stopped ringing, the quiet began to spook me. All that was left was a big cupboard. It was locked, but cheap and badly built so easy to penetrate. As I forced the lock, I had a Hitchcockian image of a body tumbling out into my arms, and suppressed a shudder.

So the forty-odd pairs of shoes I liberated were a bit of an anticlimax. Frivolous shoes with high heels and thin straps, insouciant Italian loafers, prim schoolgirls' lace-ups, ideologically-sound Chinese cloth shoes, sensible sandals and one pair of raffish tan suede boots. My first shoe fetishist: Havelock Ellis, eat your heart out.

But where did he get them?

Amid shrieks of relieved laughter, Rosie later enlightened me.

Someone had been crawling around the library under the desks stealing the shoes that girls kicked off when they were studying. Some had been subjected to unmentionable practices and abandoned in the men's toilet; others had simply disappeared.

Before I left, I gave Rosie the photo of Claire I'd removed from Jones's wall and suggested she tip off his doctors. The shoes didn't worry me much, but I was uneasy about the virgins' gallery.

I'd searched the house and found nothing more incriminating, and the backyard was solid concrete, so it was back to the runaway theory. Dining off Lebanese takeaway in front of the TV that night, I decided I'd need to know a lot more about Claire Granger to figure out where she might have headed. Then Matthew rang me.

'Miranda says we should try to help you,' he said, grudgingly. Another victim of the pink blonde.

'So help me.'

'When I came home that night, the night she left, the yellow pages of the phone book were open, and two pages had been torn out...'

'Get on with it,' I snapped. 'What bloody pages?'

'782 and 783, arsehole!' he yelled, and slammed down the phone.

The yellow pages in question covered Dog, Dogs'–Domestic, Domestic–Door, and Door. I automatically ruled out dogs and doors; Domestic Help Services seemed most promising.

Judging by the state of Claire Granger's bedroom, she wasn't schooled in the domestic arts, in fact, she'd probably never learned how to make a bed. Somehow I couldn't see her approaching an agency for a job as a household drudge.

There were nannies agencies listed, too, but I ruled them out: Australia's ruling elite like their nannies to come complete with certificates from select English and Australian academies. Besides, spoiled brats are notoriously bad at dealing with their own kind.

That left a few agencies with mysterious names that could have indicated anything from white slaving to companioning for rich old ladies. I let my fingers do the walking. An hour later, after some decidedly odd conversations and a lot of wasted aggression on both sides, I hit on Country Life. Lengthy questioning elicited the information that they placed governesses on farflung properties.

Before I put myself through the ordeal of approaching the dragon who guarded the gates of Country Life, I rang Granger and asked if Claire would be likely to go bush.

He thought for a moment: 'She's never been west of Parramatta, but Louise's family come from the land. They had a huge property in Queensland. But what makes you think she'd go out west?'

'Elaine Shumway told her Louise committed suicide,' I said. 'She's obviously had her mother on her mind these last few months. She's not acting normally. Maybe she's out there looking for Louise's past.'

'What did Elaine tell you about the suicide?' he asked, keeping his voice carefully casual.

I didn't trust Granger, so I said: 'Nothing much, just that she'd been unhappy with her marriage and that something triggered a crisis...'

'I suppose you're wondering why I never told Claire myself,' said Granger. I waited.

When he realised I wasn't going to help, he said: 'Claire reacted so badly to her mother's death I was afraid to make it worse. I was worried about her sanity. She's a lot like her mother, and I was afraid I'd lose her too.'

The conman's first commandment, I thought: When in doubt, tell part of the truth.

'There's something else,' I said. 'I think a particular incident, some bad shock made Claire run away. Do you know what it could have been?'

'No,' he said. 'She was hurt and angry when she found out about Louise's death, but I thought she was getting over it.'

Perhaps Granger was an old-fashioned gentleman who believed in keeping a lady's name out of it. Whatever his motives, he obviously had no intention of discussing Miranda with me. What the hell, it was his money.

Country Life operated out of a hole in the wall in one of the old buildings at the bottom end of Pitt Street. Some spurious looking certificates and the flattering Annigoni portrait of the Queen of

England fought for what wall space there was, and a few pale potplants gasped out their lives in the gloom. Old copies of *Readers Digest* and *Illustrated London News* completed the ambience.

I asked the gimlet-eyed middle-aged receptionist if I could see the manager. I told her I was looking for a governess. I didn't look like a grazier, but I didn't seem to be selling anything, so she gave me the benefit of the doubt, forced her bunions back into their shoes and disappeared into an inner sanctum. The governessing business didn't look all that brisk: perhaps Jane Eyre had given the profession a bad name.

When I finally got bored with counting the fly corpses in the overhead light, I picked up a pamphlet and discovered that Country Life employed only women with teaching experience. Claire didn't have any, but Miranda did.

Miss Trigg was fiftyish, with hair that was too black, powder that was too white and the sort of all-purpose eyes that could turn from sympathy to cynicism in a flash. She looked as if she had done her training running a reform school, breaking Joan Crawford's spirit.

She turned on just enough charm to hold me if I were genuine but not enough to let me get any ideas.

'What can I do for you, Mr... she consulted her desk diary... Mr Fish?'

'I'm looking for my niece,' I said. 'And I have reason to believe she might have sought employment through your agency, Miss Trigg.'

'You understand we can't give couldn't possibly give out confidential information about our clients, Mr Fish?'

'Naturally,' I said, oozing credibility. 'I don't know how to put this, Miss Trigg. It's a delicate family matter. You see my brother-in-law and my niece had a falling out, and the girl went off without telling him where she was going. Now he's had a heart attack and wants to see his daughter. He's asked me to find her.'

I paused for dramatic effect. 'This might be the girl's last chance to see her father, Miss Trigg.'

Concern flashed across her face. She didn't want to be mixed up in as messy affair like death; it would be had for business. 'And what is your niece's name, Mr Fish?'

'Miranda Marshall,' I said, taking a very long shot. If Claire Granger were travelling under her own name, I'd just blown any chance of getting information out of Miss Trigg.

Miss Trigg stared at me for a long time, obviously unable to believe a yob like me could have a well-bred, nicely-spoken niece like Miranda Marshall.

'Your niece did seem under a little strain,' she conceded finally, and went to a filing cabinet, got out a folder and gave me the details about Claire's employers.

The station, Gowrie Downs, was in south-west Queensland, on the Northern Territory border. Miss Trigg told me I'd have to fly to the nearest airport and charter a small plane; Gowrie Downs had its own airstrip. I smiled politely until I reached the hallway, where I swore loudly. Why couldn't Claire Granger have run away to Melbourne or the Gold Coast, or even Darwin?

Back at the office, I called Granger and told him where Claire was. He told me to go and get her. Then I called the McDonells at Gowrie Downs and explained the situation to the lady of the manor. I said I wanted to come to the property, break the news personally to my niece, and bring her back with me. Mrs McDonell was unamused at losing a good servant, but couldn't fault my humanitarian impulses.

Claire Granger was smart enough, and sufficiently guilty, to disguise her astonishment the next day when her uncle turned up to collect her. Mrs McDonell, like all country folk, was starved for entertainment and would have loved to witness the interview, but good manners won out, and we were left discreetly alone in the dim parlour among the dour Scottish ancestors and the heavy cedar furniture.

I'd expected some sort of emotional scene, but the girl was quite composed. Perhaps she'd had time to think, marooned thousands of miles away from her problems. Perhaps anything was better than being stuck in the back of beyond babysitting a bunch of cockies' kids.

'Are you ready to come home yet?' I asked.

'There's not much point staying now everyone knows where I am.'

'Everyone?'

'You know who I mean. My father. Miranda. Besides, I can't very well stay here now, can I? It would look pretty strange if I refused to go home to see my dying father.'

I laughed, and Claire gave me a warning glance and pointed at the door. Mrs McDonell was evidently the sort of employer who liked to stay up to date on her employees' affairs.

As if on cue, Mrs McDonell, preceded by a discreet tap on the door, entered with tea and scones to see how poor little Miranda was taking the bad news. Claire quickly raised a Kleenex to her eyes. A month in the country had done her a world of good. She had lost the dying heroine look, had tanned up, and had obviously learned to defend herself against the McDonell clan. But had she learned to defend herself against her father and Miranda?

The girl cheered up when we got out of Gowrie Downs airspace and away from Mrs McDonell's avid, solicitous looks. I asked her what her first taste of work experience had been like.

'Awful,' she said. 'They're so mean. I didn't realise people with so much money could be so mingy. Those unspeakable children. And they told me not to fraternise with any of the stockmen, particularly the Aborigines.'

As we seemed to be getting along reasonably well, I popped the big question: What had happened between her and Miranda?

'How much of the Granger family business do you already know, Mr Fish?'

'Enough.'

'Then you might as well hear the rest. Miranda is pregnant. She and my father are getting married. Miranda is going to be my stepmother.' It was said in a perfectly controlled voice. The girl had grown up in the last three months.

She looked at me: 'Are you surprised?'

'Yeah, I'm surprised.'

'Why?'

'Well, Miranda is a good looking woman, but I don't see her as a professor's wife, somehow.'

'And I can't quite see her as my mother,' said the girl.

'What are you going to do?'

'I'll move in with Rosie Blake and finish my degree. I come into my mother's money when I turn twenty-one, so I'll go to the

States and stay with the Shumways when they go back. I liked Elaine.'

'And she can tell you about your mother,' I said.

She threw me a surprised look, as if a frog had suddenly spoken. 'Yes. I'd like to know what my mother was like before...' Her voice broke. She'd hardened her heart against her father, but the mention of her mother still hurt.

'Before she married your father?'

'Before my father drove her mad,' she said, her voice stony. 'I want to know what she was like when she was my age. When she was happy.'

'So you won't marry the wrong man?'

She smiled, without humour. 'I won't marry. Ever. I just want to understand.'

Looking into those enormous, deep brown eyes, I believed her. After David Granger, no man was ever going to break Claire Granger's heart, but I suspected many would find out the hard way.

BOOM TOWN BLUES

I crept up behind the tall, elegant, dark-haired woman, grabbed her by the arse, put one arm around her waist and kissed her on the back of the neck. She wheeled around, boxed my ears, leapt backwards, eyes blazing and said 'Get your hands off me, you... God, you!'

It wasn't quite the welcome I'd been expecting. After all, I'd once done this lady quite a favour, and we'd become friends. Or so I'd thought.

Meanwhile, she was staring at me as if I were a pile of dog droppings on the boutique's expensive pale pink carpet. When she said: 'Did my husband send you?' I realised my mistake. Wrong twin.

The last time I'd seen Margaret Kincaid Cromer she was a politician's troublesome wife, and I was still one of her husband's bully boys. Now she was a glamorous Gold Coast businesswoman. Fat Barry's hundred grand had bought her a veneer of sophistication, but the threat of her husband's reappearance could still spook her.

Time to set the record straight. 'No, I'm not with him, I mean I'm not working for him now.'

'You aren't on Barry's staff anymore?'

'No, I'm a private investigator. After I resigned from your husband's office, I set up for myself.'

'But what are you doing here on the Gold Coast?'

'Watching somebody else's husband,' I said. 'A divorce case.'

The look on her face told me I'd just dug my grave a metre

deeper, so I tried to explain: 'Mrs Cromer, I'm sorry. It was an honest mistake. I thought you were Katy.'

A flush that just might have been pleasure warmed her cheeks. It was followed by cold-eyed disapproval: 'I didn't know you'd met my sister.' That meant she was still in the dark about my role in Katy's plot against her husband. I played along.

'We met in Sydney, when she was down on business,' I said.

'Oh,' she said, and I could see her wondering where on earth her sister could have run into a lowlife like me. It wasn't my place to tell her I was a saint compared to some of the 'company directors' listed in Katy Kincaid's filofax.

We smiled at each other for a while, tongue-tied: the only things we had in common were Fat Barry and Sister Kate, and both subjects were minefields. Then she snapped out of it and said: 'Kathleen is in Brisbane till tomorrow. Would you like me to give her a message?'

'Just tell her I'm in town and I'll call her before I leave.'

At I reached the door she said: 'Mr Fish, nobody ever resigned from Barry Cromer's staff. He never gave them the chance.'

I laughed. The lady was sharp. She probably always had been, but minders usually treat politicians' wives like half-witted children, and I'd been no exception.

Normally, nothing on earth would induce me to visit the Gold Coast. A friend who grew up there insists it really was a paradise once, with miles of pristine beaches, fibro holiday houses and a *mañana* mentality. The rot had set in in the sixties, he maintained, when a progressive mayor brought in meter maids and started duchessing the developers.

Now the high-rises overshadow the beaches, king tides have eaten away the shoreline and the council has to truck in sand, and the conmen outnumber the surfers ten to one. The high-rise apartments and canal developments are full of bored, bewildered oldies lured north by the lack of death duties, the sunshine and the ersatz glamour. Drifters, drug addicts, kids on the run, girls on the make and various other victims and predators eke out a precarious existence on the fringes.

Sometimes it seems like everybody you ever hated has moved there.

But while the coast might be disappearing into the sea, there's still plenty of gold around. The Gold Coast has a frontier feel; it's the sort of society where you can be born again, discarding your old skin and choosing a new mask at the border. Nobody asks questions, and personal worth is judged on the make of your car and the label on your tee shirt rather than on the state of your soul.

What can you say about a place like the Coast except that its creators made it in their own image and likeness, and it was created by property developers.

It was a Sydney property developer's wife who was paying my way to the Gold Coast. Marika Martens suspected her husband was shacking up with a girlfriend on his increasingly frequent forays north. If she were on the way out, Mrs Martens wanted to know so she could file for divorce, get his assets frozen, and clean up. Absolute secrecy was essential in case he twigged and started sending his money offshore, hiding it in the cracks in the Companies Act or syphoning it off to some bimbo.

I don't usually do divorce work, but I made an exception because it would be a public service to divest Karl Martens of some of his ill-gotten gains — even to a harpy like his wife — and besides, the job would finally get me to the Gold Coast, where Katy Kincaid, of the ironic ice-blue eyes and wicked laugh, owned an expensive dress shop.

'Syd!' shrieked Katy Kincaid, when I rang the next morning. 'When will I see you?'

'I can meet you for lunch or after closing, if you like,' I said.

She paused: 'Wait on a minute will you?' She put her hand over the phone and I could hear her talking to someone.

'Could you meet me at The Palms restaurant at about twelve thirty? Margaret wants to talk to you.'

I groaned. 'God, is she still pissed off at me for grabbing her arse?'

'It's nothing like that. She's worried. She's got a little problem.'

'Cromer?'

'We don't know. We're hoping you'll help us find out.'

How could I resist?

Every eye in the room was on me when I joined the Kincaid women at the chic Palms restaurant. The twins, with their perfect skin, rich-girl haircuts, pastel linen and discreet gold, were every male tourist's dream souvenir.

Katy leapt up and gave me a hug. 'Syd, you look... terrible,' she said and laughed.

I checked out my wrinkled suit and pasty complexion in the mirrored walls and had to agree: I'd have to get some sun while I was here.

'You look... well,' I replied.

'Oh, no. That means I'm getting fat!'

Far from it, she was glowing and sleek. She looked like a woman with a good lover.

'How's your love life?' I asked, and she blushed slightly, frowned and flicked her eyes in her sister's direction.

I desisted and ordered a scotch. The ladies were drinking daquiris which matched their clothes.

The waiter, a superannuated Kiwi surfie, goggled when he saw the Kincaids: one of his fantasies had finally come to life.

'Would it be too much trouble for you to take our order?' I asked, and he gave me a look that probably scared them silly in Christchurch.

The women ordered designer salads and I asked for a hamburger with the lot and we made small talk. When we'd exhausted the price of real estate on the Gold Coast, I asked what it was all about.

'It's Margaret,' said Katy. 'Somebody's following her. That's why she got such a shock when you turned up.'

'I want to know if it's Barry,' interrupted her sister. 'He's been too generous. I'm waiting for the backlash. I don't trust him.'

She obviously didn't know her sister and I had had to turn Barry upside down to shake the hundred grand out of his pocket. 'Are you sure it's your husband?' I asked. Have you got any other enemies? Have you knocked back any gigolos lately?' This for the benefit of the hovering waiter who coloured and crashed plates.

She laughed. 'Not that I know of. I lead a pretty quiet life, really. Kathleen is the high-profile member of the family.'

'Any men in your life?'

She hesitated.

'Marg is being courted by Jack Morgan, a local builder and developer,' her sister put in. 'A pillar of the community. Handsome, very well connected, and not married — an endangered species.'

'Is he jealous?' I asked.

'I don't think so...' she turned to her sister for help. 'Is Jack the jealous type?'

Katy shrugged. 'He's always very charming to me, but I can't pretend to know anything about him.'

'How serious is it?' I probed.

'He wants to marry me,' said Margaret.

'Do you... reciprocate his feelings?'

'I'm not sure. I've been enjoying being my own boss for the first time in fifteen years, without Barry treating me like a moron. I suppose I haven't really been all that keen to take another chance.'

'So who's following you?'

'This creepy Greek-looking guy. Very young. Looks like something out of *Miami Vice*.'

'You want me to find out who he's working for?'

She nodded.

'Before I take this on, Margaret, do you... uh, do you have anything in your life you'd rather not come out?'

She flushed violently and looked at her sister beseechingly.

'Marg, um, had a bit of a fling with a rather beautiful MYM when she first got here.'

'MYM?'

'Much younger man.'

I laughed. 'Is he still on the scene?'

'No, I decided it was undignified.'

Her sister snorted. 'More fool you. He's a cosmetic surgeon, a real spunk. And he's still hanging around waiting for her to come to her senses.'

He sounded like a good bet to me. Plastic surgery would be regarded as an essential service in this town, and he'd be loaded.

As we left the restaurant, she took my arm: 'Don't look now, but he's across the road, in that green sports car. You can see him in the shop window.'

The shadow followed us back to the shop, decided Margaret was firmly ensconced for the afternoon and left.

'He'll be back to escort me home and wait outside to see if I go out, then leave about 11 p.m.' she told me.

We decided I'd borrow Katy's car later that night and tail the Greek. There was always the possibility he'd lead me to his client; failing that he'd go home and I'd drop in on him and ask him a few pointed questions.

In the meantime, I had a living to earn. Reluctantly I went and staked out Karl Martens' office and followed him back that evening to a penthouse apartment at a high-priced address his wife didn't know about. Twenty bucks to the caretaker, a bossy Pom born to be a prison officer, told me that a Miss Linda Lacey, a blackjack dealer at Jupiter's Casino, lived there.

'She have many male visitors?' I asked.

He got the message: there was no way a blackjack dealer's pay would cover the rent of that apartment. 'We don't have nothing like that going on in this building,' he protested.

I pretended to swallow that: 'She must have a boyfriend, though?'

'It could cost me my job, gossiping about the tenants,' he said, 'But I will say this: she's a right bitch. Mean as cat shit. Never tips at Christmas or nothing. Just a little scrubber. What's this all about, anyway?'

'Divorce case,' I said. 'She might be boffing the husband of my client.'

I held out a fifty dollar note folded between my fingers. It mesmerised him. 'Now that you mention it, a middle-aged foreign looking geezer comes in fairly regularly for a week at a time, like,' he said, never taking his eye off the main chance.

'You won't have no trouble getting evidence. They go out to dinner every night, then he picks her up from the casino. Flaunts it, he does.'

I retired to the street to wait. Sprawled in the car listening to retrorock on the radio, I noticed an old bloke on a nearby balcony watching me. Our eyes met, then he went indoors. Five minutes later he emerged from the apartment building and stuck his head in the passenger window. I ignored him.

He cleared his throat loudly: 'If you don't move on I'll call the police.'

Close up, he had eyes likes oysters with winter virus, and bad breath. I tried to hold mine and talk at the same time: it made me sound like a deflating balloon.

'I know this is a bloody police state, mate,' I said, 'but sitting in your car in a residential street isn't against the law yet, is it?'

'I'm the block captain for Neighbourhood Watch. We don't like strangers hanging about.'

'What are you going to do, make a citizen's arrest, grandpa?'

He went brick red and spluttered. Not wanting him to have a heart attack on my time, I flashed my licence.

His eyes popped. 'A private detective! What are you doing here?'

I figured snoops should stick together. 'Take the weight off your feet,' I said, opening the door.

Thrilled, he climbed in. He'd bore the duffers at the golf club to death for a month on the strength of this. I pointed to the building across the road: 'I'm working for a wife. The blond blackjack dealer in the penthouse might be about to run off with her husband. Know anything about her?'

'Is he the middle-aged sugar daddy?'

'Yes.'

'Well, she's making a fool of him. She has men in and out of there all the time when he's not in town. I'm almost certain she's a call girl.'

Catching my look, he huffed: 'At my age you don't sleep much.'

I nodded sympathetically and he subsided. Then he noticed the time and said he had to go, his favourite TV show was coming on. I wondered how he got time to watch television with so much live theatre going on. I was beginning to understand why the oldies came here.

Sure enough, at seven thirty Martens emerged from the apartments with a flashy blond showgirl type with fabulous legs, silicon-enriched breasts and clothes that made the most of them, and they drove off in an LTD. Men are creatures of habit: the bimbo was a younger version of the wife.

The Martens case seemed open and shut; all I needed now were some incriminating photographs and I had him. It was early, so I stopped off at the recently refurbished Surfers Paradise Beer Garden, sank a couple of pots of Fourex, caught up on the local talent and demolished a large portion of Queensland beef. Then I wheeled down to Margaret Kincaid's apartment in Broadbeach.

The Greek was on duty, slouched down in his Triumph. The faint soulless thump of disco music reached my ears as I drove past. I took up a post down the block and waited. Sharp on eleven he pulled out and headed south. I didn't know the territory but I was lucky, the traffic was light. We travelled through miles of gaudy neon motel signs to Surfers Paradise and beyond, and he turned into Bundall, an industrial area. I dropped back.

He cruised the deserted streets, then doubled back to a building called GoldCo Construction Pty Limited. I drove on, parked around the corner, ditched the car and watched him from the shelter of a brick wall. By this time the Greek was out of his car surveying the street. Seeing nothing moving, he strolled up to the entrance, picked the lock and disappeared inside.

As he was in and out in about ten minutes, he obviously knew what he was looking for. It was a long cardboard cylinder.

He stowed it carefully in the back seat and off we went. Back to Surfers Paradise. Suffering from an overdose of protein, I was hoping he'd go home to bed, but the next port of call was the Bamboo Bar, where he made a phone call and sat down with a drink to wait.

The bar, which had seen better days, was decked out with beaded curtains, palm trees and bamboo bar stools. All it needed was Claude Rains in a soiled white suit slumped over a Singapore Sling. It was so fashionably gloomy I could have sat in his lap and he wouldn't have recognised me the next day. Fifteen minutes later his company arrived.

He was straight out of GQ's summer holiday edition — slim, dark and piss-elegant, wearing an unstructured beige linen suit, cream silk shirt, thin raspberry tie and oxblood shoes. I wondered where he'd left his panama hat. Only a furtive air marred the image. The Greek acted as if he wanted to make a night of it but the client declined a drink, handed over what looked like money and departed with the goods.

I had a choice here — follow the thief home and squeeze him a little, or find out what sort of scam these two were running. The Greek would keep: I left him counting his money in the bar and tailed the client, who cabbed it to a glitzy new hotel in Cavill Avenue. Abandoning the car in a no parking zone, I took off after him into the marble and chrome lobby and stuck with him as he pushed the lift button for the fifteenth floor. I pushed fourteen and we rose skywards. He was nervous: that was good. I got out at my floor and ran up the stairs to see him disappearing into room 1512.

I gave him five minutes. He opened the door reluctantly at my knock. I told him I was hotel security, flashed my licence and pushed him backwards into the room before he had a chance to object. There was a suitcase on the bed; he was making a quick getaway. The name tag read David J. Durham, Principal, Durham, Hardy, Jamison, Architects.

At this point all the stuff he'd learned at university about civil liberties came to his aid, and he demanded to see my ID again.

I said: 'Don't let's be unfriendly. I'm tired. I've just driven all the way here from Bundall.' I watched his face. 'GoldCo Construction.'

As the shock of being manhandled had temporarily ruptured the connection between the man's brain and his mouth, I took advantage of the lull: 'I saw the Greek liberate some plans from the offices of GoldCo Construction tonight. I followed him to the Bamboo Bar and saw him hand them over to you. You could say I've got you cold.'

'Who are you?' he said finally, loosening his collar with his finger.

'I'm a PI. The Greek was tailing a friend of mine. I wanted to see who was running him, and he led me to Bundall.'

'You aren't working for Jack Morgan?' he asked, relieved.

So that's who owned GoldCo. All roads seemed to lead to Jack Morgan in this town, but I was beginning to doubt he was behind the tail on Margaret Kincaid.

'No.'

He cheered up slightly: 'What do you want?'

'I thought Morgan might be having a friend of mine tailed, but I was wrong. But now I'm here, you might as well tell me why you're pinching GoldCo's plans.'

He was stung: 'I'm not stealing GoldCo's anything. I'm simply taking back something that's mine. The plans are for a village development in the hinterland — housing, golf courses, international hotels, that sort of thing. Morgan commissioned the designer drawings from us — that's Durham, Hardy, Jamison.'

He handed me a pretentious postmodern business card. 'Morgan hasn't paid up. Rumour has it he's in financial trouble. He bought up big in the boom and now he's trying to sell in the bust. It happens here all the time. That's why he was trying to screw us, I suppose. Then I found out he'd asked a local group to do the working drawings for our project.'

He looked at me indignantly, but I had no idea what he was talking about. I don't know much about architecture except that most Sydney architects have a lot to answer for. 'So?'

'What that means is that he's paid us the minimum to get the concept worked up, and now he's contracting the rest of the job out to cheaper people. The understanding was that Durham, Hardy, Jamison would do the lot. We were counting on it; we need the money.'

'How badly?'

'We're in trouble too. Last year we got a lot of work in and we expanded, got bigger offices, put people on. Some of the people we put on haven't brought in any work and one of our major clients went broke owing us a great deal of money. This doublecross was the last straw.'

'So how can you afford a place like this?' I asked, gesturing at the luxurious hotel suite.

'This? Since the pilots' dispute started they're practically giving away rooms in this town.'

'And you're just going to take the plans back to Sydney?' I asked.

'Yes. If we don't get the work, nobody else is going to.'

If that were his idea of corporate revenge, it was no wonder he was going broke.

'How badly does Morgan need these designs?'

'Very badly. He's in trouble now and he'll be worse off when his creditors find out he doesn't even have a concept any more.'

'So maybe he'd be willing to come to some arrangement about the designs,' I suggested.

He goggled like a goosed choirboy: 'Oh, no. I'm not putting myself out on that limb.'

For a moment I considered hijacking the plans and selling them to Morgan myself; then I realised I didn't particularly want to show my hand either.

'What you need is a middleman,' I said.

His face slammed like a safe door: 'What's in it for you?'

'A percentage. What are those plans worth?'

'He owes us fifty thousand dollars and we stand to lose another fifty if somebody else gets the job,' he said.

'Twenty per cent,' I said.

'That's bloody usury,' he said.

'Hardly. Bankcard is twenty three; overdrafts are twenty five and the loan shark on the corner is fifty. Take it or leave it.'

He took it. I left with Andrew Kotsopoulos's card.

Kotsopoulos turned out to be a street-smart St Kilda second-generation Greek who couldn't stand the Melbourne weather and joined the migration north. He made up in deviousness what he lacked in brains, brawn and class, but at least two of the latter would have been wasted here anyway.

The Greek was unwilling at first to put the bite on a hand he'd already bitten, but I was persuasive. I told him he had a choice of doing it for two grand or not doing it and explaining to Jack Morgan why he stole the plans in the first place. He eventually saw the logic in that. In the excitement of the game, I completely forgot to ask him who'd hired him to spy on Margaret Kincaid.

The next day was given over to four-way conferences, pacing the floor, too much coffee, outbursts of childish temper, protracted haggling and making arrangements for deliveries. Between phone calls I rang Katy and told her the shadow was off Margaret and that I'd tell her all about it later. She asked how much later, and I said what about tonight and she said fine.

That evening when we were divvying up the spoils I asked Kotsopoulos if he'd like to do a little surveillance on the Martens case and he agreed. He'd decided I wasn't such a bad guy after all. Having pocketed his share, he grinned like a dingo and refused to tell me who he'd been working for.

It was the middle of the night when the phone woke me. Full of rich food, champagne and cognac, I took a while to struggle awake and crawl over Katy Kincaid to answer it.

'Syd, come quickly! Help me!' shrieked Margaret Kincaid's voice. Then the phone was slammed down.

By this time Katy was out of bed throwing on her clothes.

'What's going on?' I asked as we sped through the night to her sister's apartment. Her knuckles were white where they gripped the wheel.

'Maybe Jack Morgan, or the Greek... I don't know. Why would they want to hurt her?'

'Why would anyone want to hurt her?' I asked, and as soon as the words were out of my mouth, I knew.

'Cromer,' we said in unison.

Katy skidded the car to a halt in the carpark and we raced through the lobby to the lift.

'Come on, come on,' she chanted.

On the twenty-third floor we could hear the sound of breaking furniture and a rhythmic banging. I wondered why the neighbours hadn't called the police. The door had already been forced open so we rushed in, me in front, and there he was, bashing a chair against the bathroom door screaming 'Come out, you bitch!' none other than Barry Cromer, MP, flower of the New South Wales Liberal Party, red-faced, liquor-affected and madder than a ram in heat.

'Bazza,' I said, then 'Bazza!' and he stopped in mid-lunge, chair above his head, and turned around.

'You!' he screamed and came for me. I pushed Katy out of the way and hurled myself at his knees in a tackle that would have warmed the heart of Brother Feeney, coach of the Marist Brothers Darlinghurst seconds. The chair took flight and smashed a mirror. We hit the wall with an almighty crash, and Cromer buckled and fell on me. The crack on the head disoriented me. Just as I was about to expire under the blubber or suffocate from the Johnny Walker fumes, he bellowed and gathered himself up for another round.

At this point Katy came back to life and threw herself on her brother-in-law, kicking and clawing. Cromer reeled back in surprise and I moved in for a king hit. He was saved from aggravated assault by the thundering of feet in the hall and the appearance of two young policemen in the doorway.

Neighbourhood Watch was alive and well in Broadbeach, too.

Cromer deflated like a runover toad. He was probably imagining tomorrow's headlines in the *Gold Coast Bulletin*; there would be no chance of hushing up this little domestic in the Nationals' heartland. And if by some miracle Labor got up in the upcoming State elections, he'd be a shot duck.

In the ensuing hush I remembered Margaret Kincaid and went and rapped on the bathroom door. 'Come out, Marg, it's Syd. And Katy.'

The door opened reluctantly and her pale face appeared: 'And the cavalry,' I said.

Post-morteming the following night at Surfers Paradise's most outrageously overpriced seafood restaurant, Margaret confirmed that Cromer had hired the Greek.

'He wanted a reconciliation,' she told us. 'He said it was because he missed me and he promised to change...'

Katy snorted.

'But I've been in touch with some of my friends all along, and they said now he was a minister he was worried that it looked bad to have this wife who'd run away to the Gold Coast. So of course I told him...'

'He was full of shit,' interrupted her sister.

'... that I had no intention of propping up his political career any more.' She stopped for breath.

'But why was he having you followed?' I asked.

'Because he had to be sure Marg wasn't running around with my disreputable friends,' said Katy. 'He didn't want any journalists unearthing a "past" at the next election.'

'But that's not the whole story,' continued Margaret. 'My spies tell me he's going to be investigated by the Independent Commission Against Corruption.'

'And he wants you there to hold his hand?'

'Well, um, it's a bit more complicated than that...'

'What Marg's trying to say is that she's got the goods on him and he's afraid she'll use them,' said Katy drily.

'Will you?' I asked. I'm an incurable optimist.

She lowered her lashes and I could see her eyes glittering. 'I might.' She smiled evilly and looked at her sister, who started to laugh: 'And then again, I might not.'

More fiction from
ALLEN & UNWIN

MURDER BY THE BOOK
Jennifer Rowe

New in paperback

From the author of the bestselling whodunit *Grim Pickings*, comes another fascinating mystery, this time set in an Australian publishing house.

'Of the "unable to put down" school and one which puts its author firmly into the first ranks of mystery writers.' **Daily Telegraph**

'A first rate yarn that will please the fans of the traditional murder mystery.' **Canberra Times**

FATAL REUNION
Claire McNab

The second Detective Inspector Carol Ashton mystery

Beneath the glossy exteriors of high-priced Sydney is a darker world of passion, selfishness and possession. Called in on a case uncomfortably close to home, Detective Inspector Carol Ashton struggles to remain objective when the competing demands of loyalty and desire threaten her usually cool judgement and take her closer to losing the woman she most loves.

Claire McNab is also the author of *Lessons in Murder*.

First Australian and New Zealand publication

THE CASE OF THE CHINESE BOXES
Marele Day

Claudia Valentine is back!

Claudia Valentine, Australia's original female private eye, is back — in an adventure even more intriguing than her first.

The Great Chinese Take-Away starts with a bang, for the contents of the lost safety boxes are infinitely more valuable than money. Claudia's hunt for an elaborate key leads her into a world of ancient treasures, Triad killings and decidedly disturbing kidnappings. The odd respite in a pub, or even in a confessional, seems no more than Claudia deserves.

Marele Day also writes short stories and is the author of *The Life and Crimes of Harry Lavender*.

TIGER COUNTRY
Penelope Rowe

Richly rewarding reading

Tiger Country is that rare treasure: a novel which is intellectually engaging while also exploring complex emotional issues. It moves between past and present, unravelling the effects on a woman's life of growing up in a patriarchal Catholic family where the inevitable human ambivalence about growth and change must be rigidly repressed.

Tiger Country is Penelope Rowe's second novel. She is also a successful writer of short stories.

PAINTED WOMAN
Sue Woolfe

Now in paperback

'An exquisitely intense book... This is such a robust, unpitying and honest writing about women that it becomes writing for everyone.' Thomas Keneally

Sue Woolfe has, with *Painted Woman*, established herself as a novelist of the first rank. Commentary on a woman artist's life in the present explodes with new meanings as her past is revealed—dominated by her father, *the* artist, and her dead mother, *an* artist.

CRIMES FOR A SUMMER CHRISTMAS
Edited by Stephen Knight

An immensely entertaining collection of new Australian crime stories from top crime writers, as well as top 'literary' writers new to crime: Peter Corris, Marele Day, Garry Disher, Marion Halligan, Robert Hood, Elizabeth Jolley, Nigel Krauth, Martin Long, Ian Moffitt, Mudrooroo Narogin, John Sligo, Kate Stephens, Michael Wilding and Renate Yates.

This exceptional collection of stories has been orchestrated and introduced by Stephen Knight, Professor of English at the University of Melbourne, and long-term crime writing advocate.

OCEANA FINE
Tom Flood

The *Australian*/Vogel and Miles Franklin Award winner in 1990.

A tantalising first novel dealing with multiplicity of perception — through history and memory, national mythologies, families and writing (blood and ink) puzzles and their reasons — which might be said to be their execution.

'From realism to surrealism, this is a novel always original, exciting, different.' **Geoffrey Dutton**

'An extraordinarily passionate book.' **Brian Matthews**

'An astonishing first novel.' **A. P. Riemer**

THEATRE DAZE
Colin Golvan

A comedy of modern theatrical manners

'The Perfect Moment' may well be the worst play in the world but does that mean its creator, humble Roger Normandy, deserves the treatment meted out by the giant egos striding Melbourne Repertory Theatre?

Colin Golvan, himself a playwright and barrister, has bravely faced all the sacred cows of theatre and created a short, very funny book of unrestrained irreverence — in the best tradition of Australian comic writing.

JF WAS HERE
Nigel Krauth

A major new novel from a leading Australian writer.

AIDS is killing John Freeman. From the Hydro Majestic Hotel in the Blue Mountains, JF recalls not only his own adult life, lived largely in contemporary Papua New Guinea, but also the life of his grandmother, an eccentric golf champion who, like John, paid a considerable price for the right to be 'her own person'.

JF Was Here is a novel of maturity and depth from the prize-winning author of *Matilda, My Darling* and *The Bathing Machine Called the Twentieth Century*.